Mary Andrews Denison

Ruth Margerie

a romance of the revolt of 1689

Mary Andrews Denison

Ruth Margerie
a romance of the revolt of 1689

ISBN/EAN: 9783741114816

Manufactured in Europe, USA, Canada, Australia, Japa

Cover: Foto ©Andreas Hilbeck / pixelio.de

Manufactured and distributed by brebook publishing software
(www.brebook.com)

Mary Andrews Denison

Ruth Margerie

RUTH MARGERIE:

A Romance of the Revolt of 1689.

LONDON:

GEORGE ROUTLEDGE AND SONS,

THE BROADWAY, LUDGATE.

BEADLE'S
AMERICAN LIBRARY

SIX PENCE

THE CHOICEST WORKS OF THE MOST POPULAR AUTHORS

RUTH MARGERIE

GEO. ROUTLEDGE & SONS, THE BROADWAY, LUDGATE.

RUTH MARGERIE:

A ROMANCE OF THE REVOLT OF 1689.

CHAPTER I.

RUTH AND THE TWO CAPTAINS.

In a comfortable room of the old Red Lion tavern, of ancient Boston, sat a thoughtful-looking man, busily engaged with his pen. Gigantic irons garnished the huge fireplace. The walls, bare of paper, were hung with tawdry prints. The chairs were narrow, high-backed and uncomfortable ; carpet there was none. Out of the windows, whose gray-blue panes were cased with lead, the man occasionally glanced with an expression of interest, blended sometimes with a little quiet mirth. Then, turning again to the table, he wrote what we shall here take the liberty to transcribe :—

"*From Godfrey Lamb to his Wife in Lunnon.*
"DATED BOSTON, February, 168—.

"MINE OWN DEARE WIFE :—Through ye blessing of God, I haste to tell thee of my safe arrival in this outlandish port. No misfortune happened on our vessel, save that we had an ugly passenger, whose impertinence caused ye captain and officers some trouble—and may yet work more.

"I hear that ye 'Three Pollies,' in which my goods were shipped, hath gone to ye bottom—bad luck to it—but better that I didn't go in her else had I lain at ye bottom, alsoe, with my poor goods. I only care for my golden edition—that one with ye rare illustrations, w'h cannot be matched in all England, I fear.

"I was not sea-sick in ye least, so thou cans not laugh at me, as thou didst hope to, fair lady. We met whales—monstrous ones—and sometimes white and beautiful birds, such as fly

over ocean, came within fair gun-shot—but thou knowest I
am always loath to shoot a bird, and ye sailors were too
superstitious.

"Now for this same citie of Boston!

"It bids fair to be verie goodlie.   'Tis builded on ye south-
west side of a bay, in ye w'h five hundred ships might anchor.
Ye buildings are handsome, joyninge one to another, as in
Lunnon.   Ye streets are of good size, and manie of them paved
with cobble-stone.   Ye towne is not divided into parishes, and
hath a pleasant mingling of trees and field, and a beautiful
outlook upon divers islands, on w'h I am told are gardens and
fair farms.   Toe day ye Governor arrives from New York,
w'h is now added to hys care.   Ye people here made as great
a time at ye proclamation as most of them do to-day.

"I stop, at ye present, at a famous good tavern, called ye Red
Lion.   Mistress Bean, ye landlady, is a clever sort of bodie,
verie accommodating and tidy.   She hath a little maid in her
house about whom there seems to be some commotion at this
time.   A pretty maid it is—her name Ruth—and a shame
that they should be for persecuting her!   But these American
Cromwells have no mercy.

"I had a hint ye last night from Mistress Bean, (who seems
sorry for her little maid,) that when ye captain of ye 'Prudent
Sarah' hears of it, he will take ye matter in hand.   By w'h
I should judge that ye handsome young mariner hath his eye
turned towards this star, whose light shineth now more dim
than usual.

"Ye little maid, Ruth, has just brought in my luncheon.
For all ye world she looks like thy fair niece, Mercy Apricot.
Just such soft locks curling in ripples over a fair white forehead.   Her eyes—very sorrowful and drooping—and a hope-
less look clouding over her sweet features.   She is soe handsome that even her grief maketh dimples—sad ones.

"'So, my maid,' I said, wishing to have some converse with
her, 'ye house is verie full.'

"'Yes, sir; verie full,' she made reply, in a low voice.

"'I suppose ye captain of ye 'Prudent Sarah' stops at this
tavern?' I added, to see what effect.   Well, ye red color
floated up like crimson rose leaves—fluttered all over her fair
cheeks, and up to ye verie roots of her golden hair

" The young mariner, they say, is ye most beautiful man in Boston. It is made no secret that a noble lady, by name Bellamont, is verie much in love with him. About ye little maid I will tell thee more in my next.

" I have been introduced to many persons here, and expect shortly to dine wi' ye Governor. Attended worship in ye Towne Hall, last Lord's day. Ye Reverend Parris Aldrich officiated. He is, by marriage, related to ye Governor. Ye people, of course, hate ye English service—they be soe afraid of Popery! Verie well! Sir Edmund will learn them a lesson or two.

" By ye way, mie trunk with ye black silk-velvet small-clothes got badly wetted with ye salt water. I have had to furnish myself with a new suit.

" I walked abroad last night. Ye towne seemed to me to be verie rich and populous. On ye south there is a small but pleasant ground, called ye Common, where ye gallants, a little before sundown, stroll with their marmalet maidens, as we do in Moorfields, till ye nine o'clock bell rings them home, when presentlie constables walk their rounds to see good order kept and to take up loose people.

" I smile to think how easily a bodie may here get lost. Yesterday, on asking a man where I was—bewildered—(a common fellow,) he answered, ' in Pudding Lane.' Truly, it did transport me back to Lunnon. Write me soon—dear heart. Thy   LAMB."

A full moon lighted up the waters of Boston harbor. Here and there the land jutted out, running low and shelvingly into the liquid tide, and covered to its borders with what had been summer verdure, now brown and dry. A thousand little ripples hummed ceaselessly along the shore. Here and there boats were hauled up in the shadows of the wharves, and the town, looking from this stand-point, seemed a fairy mass of silvery roof-tops, so strong were the beams of the December moon, so bright and dancing were the little flames in all the windows.

The islands in the far distance—the ships at anchor—the white wake of glistening light coming from a remote point, widening and glowing, made a fair picture—especially as the

stars, unusually thick and brilliant, were everywhere reflected
in the great ocean mirror.

A sound of oars, striking rapidly, broke the deep stillness.
Presently a boat rounded from a near cove, and was guided
fast and vigorously toward the land. Five men composed the
boat's complement—one seemed, from his manner, to be the
commander.

Cautiously nearing Boston pier, they gazed on all sides,
and very slowly and with extreme quiet, the men and their
Captain landed.

The latter stood in a careless attitude, gazing townward,
one foot on the wooden coping of the wharf. He was plainly
dressed in the sea garb of that day—heavy trunk-hose, dark
small-clothes, added to which he wore a cloth cloak and an
ordinary cap that seemed to have seen much service. Upon
his face the moon shone, revealing a thick beard, that appeared
to be artificial, for once or twice he pressed it on more securely with his hand. He had a dark, handsome, but evil face,
and wore his hair longer than was the fashion; but it was
curious to see, as he removed the cap, the curling tresses rise
with it, revealing a mass of very thick, short curls. His business was piracy, and his haunt one of the small islands in the
harbor. Though a price was set on his head, he had evaded
justice thus far, by his brazen assurance and ready wit. He
spoke, hastily:

"Now, men, two of you—Ned and Jo—carry the boat over
to Winnissimmet, and keep her quiet, unless you hear my sig-
nal. You, Abe and Hatch, stop at the Red Lion, and gather
what news you can respecting the 'Prudent Sarah.' Be particular and find out whether any of the passengers have left
their traps aboard, as I suspect they have. I shall be busy
to-night. Perhaps you may hear of me somewhere about
two or three—and I may give you news sooner."

"Ay! Cap'n;" answered the men, severally, lifting their
woolen caps.

"There's nine!" exclaimed the Captain, as a bell from the
nearest belfry rung out. "That will send the people home.
Their rejoicing over the Governor's return hasn't cost 'em
much, I should judge; it's pretty still, any way. That's a
nice looking craft, in this light," he soliloquized, turning

bayward as two men sprung into the boat in obedience to his orders. "I'd like that fine frigate in an open sea," he continued, " with plenty of pickings afloat."

The "Kingfisher," the vessel alluded to, was a fifty-gun frigate, and lay at anchor not more than half a mile from the shore. Her rigging looked drift-white, and the red mouths of her port-holes were burnished with a fiery glow. Softly a thousand slender threads of rippling light, as if drawn by invisible fingers and luminous needles, worked a delicate netting at the place where her dark hull rested on the water. Now and then sprays of soft gleams crept suddenly up her bulky sides and flashed down again, seemingly quenched in the tide.

The pirate, Captain Bill, as his men called him, moved rapidly up the wharf and disappeared. By this time another boat was seen quickly and boldly winning her way toward the place where the Captain had so lately stood. Six strong arms rowed her, and in the stern-sheets sat a young man, with a cloak folded about him. He, too, sprung out, as his predecessor had done, but with a different mien. He spoke in loud, hearty tones, and seemed glad to feel the shore. He lifted his cap, but the slightly-curling locks that just touched the handsome neck were his own, and no unduly heavy weight of hair disfigured his face.

"Well, men, it's a sharp night and you have rowed well," he said, drawing from his pocket some coin. "Here is something with which to drink confusion to the Governor. Duke, don't you get tipsy, my good fellow."

This he said addressing a small, loose-jointed man, who, in his heavy woolen roundabout and red skull-cap, stood balancing his money on one of his fingers, and who now presented a keen, cunning countenance, his one eye almost lost in the habitual wrinkles of a habitual wink.

"Ketch Catchcod, Duke of Marma, to spend his money for what steals the brains, as the poet says. Brains is a scarce commodity, and I ain't got any to spare except what I hammer into this shape ;" and, pulling at his front lock, he exclaimed in a spouting tone :

> "Thank ye, Cap'n, thank'e kindly,
> And I'll try and not go it blindly;
> For shillins isn't always to be had,
> And when they are—"

He scratched his head, crying with a look of perplexity, " I can't think of any rhyme but *bedad!*—and I don't know how to bring him in."

" That will do, Duke," said the Captain, smiling. " You can stop at the Red Lion, if you wish, with me, or go with the other men to the Blue Anchor "—laughing again at Marmaduke Catchcod's original poetry, showing his white teeth, his splendid face proving the assertion that he was the most beautiful man in Boston. Browned though he had been by the impartial sun, the elegance and regularity of his features —the soul-light sparkling in his eyes—the dimples nestling in either cheek—the dainty brown whiskers—made him most unexceptionably handsome. It was no marvel that he was admired as much by the men as the maidens, wherever he went.

The man who had improvised the nowise remarkable verse of thanks was an original phase of the Jack-tar genus. The sailors had dubbed him " Catchcod, Duke of Marma," and he was in no way displeased with the title, but rather liked it. Originally picked up in the by-streets of London by Captain Cameron, rescued from beggary if not starvation, Marmaduke was pledged, body and soul, to his kind master. On board ship, he was in many respects Captain Cameron's right-hand man, proving himself serviceable in all things. The Captain had taught him to write, and, as he was remarkably apt, after a time he became equivalent to a secretary—copying the log, and otherwise turning his talents to account. He was an indefatigable reader, catching up every thing that came in his way that promised a story. In the rough draught he was also something of a genius, and in fact he made himself of service wherever he was.

Leaving one man to take the boat back to the vessel, Captain Cameron bent his steps toward the Red Lion.

CHAPTER II.

TAVERN GOSSIP AND NEW ACQUAINTANCES.

IN all the windows of the Red Liou tavern flickered lights —some burning with a full, bright flame, others far spent and dying. Without, the noise of laughter, conversation, and the clanking of glasses fell on the ear. Iu the streets all was still, save here and there some weak-headed reveler unconsciously disturbing the peace, and preparing himself for a night of inglorious coufiuemeut.

Captain Camerou entered. Mistress Bean bustled into the hall. She was a short, firm-visaged personage, her jetty locks escaping from a full English cap, her gown of red stuff tucked up at both sides over a black petticoat. Her cheeks were apple-red, plump and round, her eyes black and restless.

"Why, Captain !" she exclaimed, "I'm master glad to see ye. Why didn't ye come before ?"

"Business, Mistress Bean ; business ! Well, I hope you are prosperiug."

"Yes, middling—more since the Governor's come," said Mistress Bean, setting her arms akimbo, while the muslin-like ribbons of ruddiest cherry gave a brighter color to her face. "La ! you should have seen the sights this afternoon ; training ain't nothin' to it, I do assure you. It was a master fine show. The procession went almost to Flounder lane, with sights of soldiers, and music and shouting. I just got the least bit glimpse of the Governor, and I assure you he looked as big and stately as King James himself. Come, Captain, do go into the parlor and take somethin', won't ye ? There's a good fire there."

Mistress Bean pauted and puffed. She was almost out of breath.

"No, thank you, mistress," replied the young ship-master ; "I'll step in the keeping-room." As he entered, his fine dark eyes roved from side to side, as if in search of some missing face, even while he received the congratulations of those whom he knew.

Groups of townsmen, drinking and discussing the movements of the day, nearly filled the long, low-ceiled room. A
few were tossing off strong potations at the famous bar of the
tavern, and were already in a state that required some attention ; but still there did not seem to be any manifestation of
riotous feeling.

In a rude way, this common apartment was decorated with
flags, and candles, and pieces of pine and hemlock trees. A
picture of King James, whose swollen cheeks suggested the
possibility of a royal toothache, hung conspicuous over the
wide •mantel, dressed in evergreen.   In the enormous fireplace, great logs sent out hissing flakes of flame, and the fire
of itself was no mean illumination.   There were prints of
ships, in manifold colors, hung here and there; the floor had
been sanded, but the rough heels of the townsmen's shoes
had made all manner of hieroglyphics in the once clean
powder that grated under foot.

Barmaid Molly—a dashing specimen of a cockney English
girl—seemed the focus to which the glances of the young
men were attracted, and her very conscious manner and brid-
ling vanity gave her a coarse individuality.   After Captain
Cameron came in, she had eyes for none beside him.   Re-
peatedly, in her nervous haste, she poured liquors out of the
wrong bottles, and as often was taken to task for not making
the right change, while the smile (curious and envious—
sheerly impertinent in some of her rude admirers,) went sig-
nificantly round.   In one corner, perched upon a stool, a
green-baize bag dangling from his shoulder, a fiddle held in
his arms as one would hold a child, sat Long Loose Benjamin, the ubiquitous.   He had already been in every tavern
in Boston, and at the eleventh hour he entertained the Red
Lion, and after playing the doleful ditty with which he
always preluded his entertainments, had set them all to
dancing, inside and out—for there are some men who, though
they think it a deadly sin to dance, go through all the motions to themselves at the sound of a merry tune.

But the bell had rung nine ; the authorities allowed nothing of the kind after that hour, so Long Loose Ben, a steeple
of bones six feet and more, sat hugging his fiddle.

The other personages who merit a particular description

stood, two of them, together, busily talking. One was a keen-eyed old man of seventy, with hair white as the driven snow and shining as silver, braided into a long cue adown the back. He stood bent over somewhat—though his natural attitude was perfectly upright—his hands crossed on the silver head of his cane. His name was Comstock—commonly he was called father Comstock. He was a bookseller, at the sign of the Blue Glove, in Union street, and a most devout as well as capable man. The other was a restless-eyed, excitable elderly man, a bricklayer, and well known and esteemed for his zeal, both in State and Church matters. To these two men the young ship-master first spoke.

" Ah, me !" and father Comstock shook his head after the salutations were passed, crossing one leather-breeched leg over the other ; " it's great times we're having now in this town, great times. The Governor can't even come from New York, but he must have a reception. The Lord save us ! He alone knows what'll come of it !"

" I s'pose thou'st heard," cried Gaffer Scates, with the eager air of a man anxious to impart the first news, " I s'pose thou'st heard that the new rector, as the church folk call him, the minister Aldrich, read prayers out of the book, in the town-house, last Sabba'day."

" Yes, and with a Popish gown on, all full of pleats and divers needlework—ah, me ! In what a guise comes the Evil One sometimes," added father Comstock.

" And that bodes no good, you think," said the Captain, with a manner as if he would be interested, yet watching the door narrowly. As he spoke, two sailors entered and went directly to the bar.

" No good ! Why, our liberties are in danger, dost see ?" exclaimed Gaffer Scates, with an authoritative gesture. " I should think, truly, it boded no good. Hither comes a tool of the Governor from England, three days agone, in the frigate ' Kingfisher,' and brings a new charter with which to cut down our freedom. Soon will there be such multitudes of taxes that we poor craftsmen can neither live nor die decently."

By this time the sailors had taken their refreshment, and were cautiously edging round to where Captain Cameron stood listening, with that strange, far-off expression on his face.

"Then there seemeth to be a stir about witchcraft. Even one of your passengers, Captain, the jewel-merchant, reported foul doings on board the 'Prudent Sarah,' during thy passage from England," said father Comstock.

"Aha!" exclaimed the young Captain, his face taking on some interest. "So that old royalist is brewing mischief! Well, let him try it, that's all; he'll find that I, for one, don't fear him."

"Why doth he bear thee such spite, master?" asked father Comstock, deliberately buttoning up his old claret coat. "They say he hath maligned thee to the Governor."

The two sailors (evidently spies) came still nearer, and, while they appeared to be intent, one upon packing down the tobacco in his clay pipe, the other deliberately surveying a coarse print, representing a sailor in a new fit-out, (a compromise between tarpaulin and roundabout, and a landsman's broadcloth, in which poor Jack looked terribly uncomfortable,) they still—now and then exchanging glances—listened with wide ears to every word that was spoken.

"Why does he bear me spite? Because we disputed about Kirke, the Governor that was to be of these Colonies, and I called him a bloody rascal, which he is!" The Captain brought one hand down into the palm of the other with tremendous force. "He being, as I understand, a relative of that accursed hound, took me to task and insisted on fighting me. To this I would not consent, stating as a reason that my principles forbade my dueling. He then gave me a violent blow, which I resented sailor-fashion: that is, I floored, or rather decked the gentleman, whichever you will, and tied him till he promised submission—and, I doubt not, himself vengeance. The old fellow embarked in England with the intention of remaining in Boston, but he swears now that he will not stay in a country where such cut-throats, as he is pleased to call me, have the rule; so I expect to take him back again. He declares, however, in his rage, that he shall return to England in the 'Prudent Sarah,' but under another Captain; with such threats he thinks to intimidate me, but I declare he shall not. If it had not been for one thing more than another, I'd have pitched his old carcass, trunks, boxes and all, out of my vessel, and sent them ashore; but I want to convince the man that the people can do something in this country—we are the king here," and he drew his handsome figure proudly up.

"Hush! hush!" said Gaffer Scates.

"Hist! hist!" said father Comstock.

"Don't be afraid, friends. I understand myself perfectly," said the young ship-master, turning round and seeing no one near, for, by twos and threes, the people had dropped out, leaving Long Lean Benjamin asleep in his corner, his nose touching the bridge of his fiddle. "He would take the law on me in a moment, but he knows it wouldn't do for him. Two other passengers saw the whole thing, and that he offered the first assault. One of them—a book-merchant of the name of Lamb—said that he should have slightly amended my act, that is, he should have thrown him overboard for the fishes. I told him I had too much pity for the poor things," he added, laughing; "they never would have digested his tough old English hide."

"It was all true, then," said Gaffer Scates, hat in hand, "that, when Monmouth was defeated, this Kirke hung men, drinking healths to the king?"

"Ay! was it true!" replied the ship-master, his brilliant eyes flashing; "thirty of them—ten turned off in a health to the king, ten to the queen, and ten to that cursed Jeffries, whom may some rascal do the same service by."

"Thy tongue is somewhat too free for thine own good, young man," said father Comstock, gently; "curb it a little—not but what thou art right—righteous indignation is not forbidden by the Scripters, I take it, and it gladdens my old heart to meet with one who loves his country, as I am sure thou dost, and whom the constant contact with other nations doth not in the least prejudice against his own. But Goody will think me lost if I do not open her front door by the stroke of ten. Let us hope that our Governor will rule well and justly—alack-a-day! if that may be—but Heaven forbid that he turn out a Papist, as has been hinted."

"The Governor!" cried the young Captain, with a sneer, and setting his lips firmly together; "he would do Kirke

over again, give him but the opportunity. It's my opinion
that we don't need these royalists to rule us. Why can't we
choose our own rulers? What do we, a people able to main-
tain ourselves and our laws, want of these princely tools of
the king, with their guards, their liveried servants, their
black-hearted secretaries, their red-coated inso—"

"I do wish the maid would come."

At this pettish voice, quite near him, the handsome young
Captain changed color, and apparently forgot his speech.

"Is it Ruth you speak of, Mistress Bean?" he asked.

"Yes; the child was called to a council, and had to go
alone, as I was overmuch busied with seeing to the strangers."

"Called to a council? What council?" cried the young
ship-master, in a tone of strong surprise.

"A church council," was the reply. "Of course you have
not heard of it. It's some doings of that Lady Anne, who,
with her fashions and her extravagances, is always getting
poor folks into trouble," said the landlady, now intent upon
shaking into consciousness Long Lean Ben, who, with a most
perverse pertinacity, only hugged his fiddle closer and snored
the louder.

"That Lady Anne doeth our young people much harm,"
said father Comstock, laying his hand on the latch of the
door. Almost at that instant the door was pushed open from
the outside.

The new-comer was one of kindly yet austere presence.
He was dressed in the precisely-fashioned garments of a
clergyman, and bore in one hand a stout cane. Following
him closely came a timid, beautiful young creature, her eyes
downcast, her head somewhat bent. Her delicate lips curved
with the impress of a great sorrow. For a moment, she
stood dejected, silent, her arms folding her thick cloak about
her in such a way that her hands pressed against her heart,
as if to keep down its heavy pulsings.

"Doctor Mather!" exclaimed father Comstock, a blending
of humility, reverence and affection in his manner, and, with
low bendings of the body, both worthies shook hands with
their minister.

"Mistress Bean," said the doctor, turning to the portly
hostess, who, in some confusion, was striving to hide the

snoring fiddler by the disposition of her portly body to that effect. "I have brought home the little maid in safety. We have been dealing with her. Thou wilt see that she hath proper time for meditation and prayer, and as much as thou canst spare. We find her very penitent, but not easy to be entreated."

The young ship-master had all this while stood quietly by, striving by every mute endeavor to catch the downcast eye of the sorrowful, beautiful girl, who still maintained an attitude of the deepest dejection. Now his eyes flashed fire as he exclaimed, with a sailor's abruptness :

"Of what crime, reverend sir, does this maiden stand accused ?"

For the first time the young creature looked up, and, encountering the passionate gleaming of the master's eye, a deep, hot crimson rushed over cheek and brow, and releasing her hands, she turned away and bent her face within them.

"Young sir ! thy manner savors of more irreverence than we could wish in one of thy age addressing a senior," said Doctor Mather, in a low, silken voice, and with unblanched dignity. "We did not speak touching any crime, if we remember. We said we had been dealing with the maiden, but made no allusion to any accusation whatever."

"Oh ! your honor—your reverence, I mean, will excuse me for not introducing this young gentleman," said Mistress Bean. "Master Cameron, Doctor Cotton Mather, our good clergyman of the new church."

The young ship-master bowed stiffly, while the doctor, standing yet more uprightly, exclaimed :

"Have we here the commander of the ship ' Prudent Sarah ?' "

"That is the name of our good vessel," replied the Captain, promptly.

"We have heard of you," said the doctor, with another rapid but more suspicious glance. "You brought passengers, some of whom we have seen."

"Yes, sir ; five passengers ; four of them gentlemen, and one a knave," said the young man, bluntly.

The reverend doctor glanced first at the undaunted Captain, then at Mistress Bean, then toward the two worthies by the door, as much as to say, " What kind of a fellow have we here ?"

" We know not to whom thou alludest," he answered, slowly ; " we, ourself, have met but two—a young merchant by the name of Lamb, and an elderly gentleman, who calls himself Obed Bentley, jeweler to the king."

" Jeweler and lickspittle, you might add, saving your reverence," said Captain Cameron, almost fiercely. " That man is a toad, and would be willing to be trod upon by a king's toe."

. Father Comstock and Gaffer Scates looked aghast at this inconsiderate speech, and Doctor Cotton Mather stood for a moment, his eyes riveted upon the beautiful, haughty face wreathing all over with indignation, with its shining eyes, broad, proud brow, and its lips curved scornfully.

" May the Lord give thee a more Christian spirit," he said, gently—so gently that the young man changed color, and became instantly as meek as he had before been defiant.

" I ask your pardon," he said, frankly ; " these things only concern myself, and I am to blame for my rashness."

CHAPTER III.

THE ANCIENT-TIME TEA-PARTY.

A PLEASANT room, facing on the street—the sunshine streaming in—and Mistress Comstock knitting by her cheerful fire. A happy and serene woman looks Mistress Comstock, and it seems as if the shining furniture reflected her placid, handsome old face. Handsome, because the royal stamp of goodness makes it so. The sunshine of her youth lingers yet on the hill-top of old age. Every thing seems as blessedly content as herself. A tabby cat, coat flaming yellow, and luxuriating in most masculine whiskers, lies purring and blinking on the ruby-red hearth. The very logs in the great fireplace seem happy because permitted to burn, and each flame appears striving to overleap its predecessor.

Comfort blithe, comfort snug, predominates. The moon-faced pewter dishes over the chimney-piece—the bright-blue tiles, portraying a pleasant Scripture story—the quaint little buffet in the corner, holding its small store of China-ware, very precious and very old—the brass-polished candlesticks, the well-waxed floor, and the goodly, black, round, three-clawed table, glistening in its nook—every thing is apparently well satisfied to be worn out, if need be, in the service of the inestimable Mistress Comstock.

"'Tis time the child was come," she murmurs, setting her needles and smoothing down her well-plaited cap. "Poor dove! I know not how to comfort her, but she shall see that there is no difference in my feelings," she adds, giving a sigh.

The words are scarcely spoken before a low rap sounds at the door, and as the cheerful old woman cries, "Enter, dear," Ruth Margerie comes in. Her eyes look heavy, and her sweet young face a little careworn, but as she sits down in a low chair at the feet of Mistress Comstock, the genial fire drives the cold from her cheeks.

"Mistress Bean sent me round to say, with her compliments, that she can not come to tea this afternoon; she would, but that her many duties forbid." All this Ruth rehearses, carefully pulling off her white wool mittens and holding forth her hands—very delicate, pretty hands they are, the old lady thinks, as the fire-flame gives them pink outline and transparent flush.

"I'm sorry," Mistress Comstock returns, placidly, "but *thou* canst stay, cosset," she adds, with a questioning, sympathizing glance at the girl, who sits watching the fire-play so mournfully.

"Oh! if you will let me,"—the words came forth as a wail, the girl, bowing her head impulsively on the lap of the kind-hearted old dame, sighs heavily, almost sobbingly.

"Let thee, dear lamb! Why shouldst thou make a speech like that to thine old friend?" and Mistress Comstock looks grieved, and, with her hands, tenderly forces the bended head upward till she sees the tear-filled eyes.

"Because—oh! because everybody treats me so coldly! so almost unkindly—yes, yes, I will say it—so cruelly, now—what will it be after—after—the Sabbath?"

She shudders from head to foot.

"My poor cosset!" cries Mistress Comstock, "if thou must bear the cross, bear it bravely, even as He did who is our salvation."

"But it is heavy—heavy!" sobs poor Ruth.

"Thou shalt find peace with me, dear child!"—the good woman's voice melts as if there were tears born of love in it. "Stay here, if thou wilt, even till thy trial is through. I doubt thee not, cosset; never, never have I doubted thee—nor has goodman Comstock. 'Twas only yesterday he spoke nobly in thy cause to the young Captain."

"Captain Cameron?" Ruth's cheek betrays the secret of her heart in the heart's own red letter—her voice is quick, but the word falls lingeringly from her lips.

"Yes, that hasty, impatient, but brave, honorable young man."

"Ah! brave, honorable!" echoes Ruth; "and he, too, noble as he is—he, too, doubts me—despises me. Well—I will try and bear it."

How meek and saint-like, yet womanly and despondingly, she looks as she says it—her voice choking at the close.

"He spoke of thee almost as if he were a sweetheart of thine," says Mistress Comstock, giving Ruth a searching glance. The young maid has turned her head a little away; she makes no answer, but her cheek feels the burning of a tear, that is silently wiped away, and the click of the needles goes on.

After a little pause, Ruth slowly disenvelopes herself of her outer garments, and hangs them up in the little passage between the lean-to and the family room. While she smooths back the curls that the high wind has disarranged, in comes Mistress Seates, with much stamping of the light, damp snow from her moccasins. Mistress Seates is a comfortable woman, fat and forty; her fair, round face abounds in dimples; her mouth and brow indicate great decision of character. It is three o'clock by the tiny old-fashioned time-piece between the windows, yet Mistress Comstock reproaches her friend with being "so late!"

With fewer apologies than are fashionable to-day, the plump visitor emerges from her envelopes, bestows a hearty kiss on the cheek of Ruth, because, " poor child !" she says in her heart, " she has no mother to kiss her in her trouble," and very soon the two dames are as busy with their tongues as they are with their knitting.

" Will you give me something to do, Mistress Comstock ?" Ruth is nervous ; her restlessness will not allow her to keep unemployed, as her hurried manner gives token.

" Child, there is nothing but what I can do myself," answers the good woman, smiling.

" Well, then, let me do what you could, please," coaxed Ruth. " Are there no cakes to bake ? no biscuit to make ? There is the tea to draw and the table to set. Why won't you sit still and let me work ? It will make me happier."

The quiver of the lip decides it for Ruth.

" Well, cosset, have thy way. The dough is ready for the bread, and the oven is hot. Thou mayst do all, if it will please thee, child, and I'll play lady for once," returns the good dame. " The damask cover is in the top drawer of the chest, where, also, thou wilt find six spoons of silver. Would I had more, but we home bodies can use the pewter. In the second drawer, cosset, is my Chiny tea-caddy. Three tops to a drawing, dear—it is not often that we have tea, and we must make it of the strongest. Thou wilt find cream and sugar in the buttery—the sugar in a strong box, which may tax thy strength to open, as father and I never eat it. The butter, in which I had very good luck this morning, (a beautiful churn-ing, Mistress Seates,) in the pantry, in the stone jar—and my preserves thou knowest about."

Ruth, trying to remember her instructions, goes into the lean-to, or kitchen, and is soon busy with the biscuit, while Mistress Comstock and Mistress Seates gossip to their hearts' content.

" Never pitied I poor maid so thoroughly," says Mistress Comstock, softly.

" It is all very sad," replies the other, shaking her head till her double chin quivers like jelly. " Our good minister told me that he knew not what to make of the case."

" Depend upon it, the poor maid is innocent," replies Mis-tress Comstock.

" Ah ! Mistress, I think so too—but it's a wicked, wicked

world—a very wicked world,"—and the double chin quivers again, (a reminder of colorless jelly,) but this time with a wise and long-drawn sigh.

"Dost thou know aught of the ship-master, Cameron?" inquired Mistress Comstock.

"I have seen him. He hath the usual vanity of man," is the sententious reply.

"Shall I set the table now, Mistress Comstock?"

Ruth looked like her own lovely self as she put her bright face in at that moment. The pretty cheeks were flushed with exercise, and the flush brightened the blue eyes. Mistress Scates thought it couldn't be time, and then exclaimed, as she saw the hand of the clock pointing to five, that she had not deemed it scarce an hour since she sat down.

The table soon stood in the center of the company-room, as it was called in those times, and Mistress Comstock's array of China made a fine show on the damask cover. An ordinary June rose would have filled either of the red-tinted cups, while a moderate handful of rose-buds might have brimmed the quaint sugar-bowl—as assuredly half of that quantity would have run over the top of the tiny creamer. The cream, however, stood near in a homely jug of brown delf. Scarcely was the table finished, and Ruth in the lean-to, preparing to take the smoking cakes from the oven, when in came father Comstock with a stranger, followed by Gaffer Scates and Captain Cameron.

Ruth heard the latter's voice—she started—and her face assumed an expression of deep distress. She had not dreamed of seeing him—had avoided him since that last painful interview.

"Oh! if I had but known!" she repeated to herself, standing there undecided what to do. In her desperation she would have thrown on Mistress Comstock's old hood and cloak and fled from the house, but at that moment the old lady herself came into the lean-to.

"Oh! do they know I am here?—because if not, let me go home at once," cried Ruth, while her disordered manner struck the good dame unpleasantly, and she answered, almost sharply:

"Of a surety they do, child; for I just now said to father

that Ruth had been kind enough to serve me, and would bring in the tea soon."

"Can't I stay here—won't it be better? Don't ask me to go in; I can't face the—the—gentlemen."

"Why, Ruth, that would look like guilt, surely," said Mistress Comstock, in a voice sterner than was her wont, and with a grave, suspicious countenance.

With her usual habit of meek submission, when counseled by her elders, Ruth dried the tears on her lashes, and, calling up all the resolution she could command, went, with downcast eyes and blushing cheeks, into the room.

"She never looked so pretty in all her life," said Mistress Comstock to herself; "and how little she knows it."

Captain Cameron now started, and his chest began to heave with long breaths, while his eyes followed her, and Mistress Scates afterward averred that he clenched his teeth hard.

Ruth, with a graceful courtesy to the company, (though her sight was dazed, and she really saw no one,) vanished again into the kitchen. Then the Captain's senses seemed to return, but not his wit and brilliancy. Through the whole tea-time (Mistress Scates again) the Captain kept looking toward Ruth, though exactly like a man who was not conscious of what he was doing; and sometimes Ruth was rosy and sometimes pale.

Suddenly a loud, important rap at the outer entrance arrested the general attention. Goodman Comstock hurried to the door, and presently returned with some haste, ushering into the room no less a personage than the stately, haughty secretary of his Excellency, Governor Andros.

Bestowing a formal salutation on the company, most of whom had arisen at his entrance, and stood now, a little awed perhaps at his velvet and finery, his glittering sword-handle and golden chain, his embroidered waistcoat and ruffled sleeves, he turned himself about, saying, as he addressed the bricklayer:

'This is Gaffer Scates, I presume? I am deputed by his Excellency, the Governor-General, to say to thee, it is his wish that thou dost deliver to him the key of the South Church, that he, in company with the many of his like faith in this

town, may have services read there on the ensuing Sabbath."

"Insolence!" muttered Captain Cameron, in a contemptuous voice.

"Thou'ast better hold thy tongue, sirrah!" exclaimed the
secretary, a tremor of passion running through the calm of
his tones; "already thou art an object of very marked suspicion. One would think the nails of thy church were of solid
gold."

"Nay, but our principles are something more solid than
that—ay! and infinitely more precious," returned father Comstock.

"Very well—we do not threaten," said the secretary,
"but if harm come to thee, remember it might have been
averted."

So saying, he strode indignantly from the room, his message
ineffectual.

Mistress Comstock entered, and spoke in a low voice to her
husband.

"Is Miss Ruth ready to go?" asked Captain Cameron, divin-
ing her errand; "because, if she is, *I* will see her to the Red
Lion."

There was no answer. The two women exchanged mean-
ing glances, and father Comstock said, after a long pause,
during which the Captain was putting on his overcoat, "Perhaps it is the maiden's wish—"

"I shall see her to the Red Lion," said the Captain, with
emphasis, breaking in upon his sentence, and there were but
few words spoken till after the two were gone—for Ruth, in
fact, was allowed no choice. Then—*perhaps* there was a little
scandal.

CHAPTER IV.

RUTH'S GREAT TROUBLE.

THE Captain and Ruth arrived at the tavern, and as yet no word had been spoken. They stood in the dim parlor alone.

"Ruth! Ruth!" he cried, softly. She did not answer.

"Ruth, you will at least speak to me. Wait a moment; only a moment—come in here—there is a light. Oh! Ruth, you will give me one minute."

"Oh! Captain Cameron!"

Ruth said this in a distressed way, as she paused. His imploring tones moved her heart to its very depths; and yet that heart was almost breaking because of her grief—because of him. How could she face him in the darkness of the anguish that had been thrust upon her?

"Ruth, will you not tell me what the trouble is—me, who have a right to know and a will to counsel? You are suffering—suffering alone. I must believe you are innocent, Ruth, whatever imputation they cast upon you."

"Oh! bless you for that! bless you for that!" she cried eagerly, excitedly, clasping her small hands together.

She had taken her hood off, and now Captain Cameron stood stroking, as with a woman's gentle hand, her soft, golden hair, and waiting till she should speak. At last she checked the tears and the pitiful sighs, and, resting her bended brow on both hands, seemed gathering courage to speak.

"It all happened last week."

This was the way she commenced, and in a voice so low and sad that the handsome young Captain thought to himself it was like the wailing undertone of the first sound of a storm just breaking over the deep.

"Ruth, my darling!" he murmured, in a voice subdued, but full of feeling.

Instantly the short-lived quiet died out of her manner, and her head was bowed again—she struggling with her tears.

"Come, now, tell me what was the accusation? Was it so terrible?" he asked, with a bantering voice.

"Oh! I can not! I can not!" she cried, writhing.   "And yet you must know—you will hear—everybody will hear and talk of it—and I shall die—I shall die of shame!"

She said this in such utter agony of tone and manner, that the young man stood gazing upon her in astonishment.

"Why, Ruth! is it so serious as that?   Has any one dared to cast an imputation on your good name?   Because, if so!" —his lips came together again—his eyes were full of indignant fire.

"It happened—it *did* happen—I did meet him—he did kiss me—it is true—all true—but—" she drew one heavy breath, shuddered from head to foot, and the sobbing voice was silent.

"*He!*—Who?   Kissed you, did you say?   Kissed *you*, Ruth—*you*, Ruth?"

There was power like that of the heavy-toned thunder in the man's suppressed voice.   He stood off at arm's-length, looking at her from under his knit brows.

"It is true," she answered, in a faint voice, from which all freshness, all elasticity had gone.   "Oh! Captain Cameron— you, too, will no longer be my friend, for I can not tell even you."

"Can not tell!   What does it mean, Ruth?   Only tell me what it means," he asked, going toward her.   "You say you met *him;* met *who*, Ruth?"

She shook her head; scalding tears fell over her cheeks, but did not disfigure the pure, beautiful face.

"I can not tell you any more than I could tell the council —that if they could have patience—only have patience—for what time I know not—they should learn every thing," she said, as if she accepted his mistrust meekly.   "It is no use to ask me; I must die before I tell."

"When did you meet this man?" asked Captain Cameron, with forced calmness.

"Last week—last week, on Tuesday night," she replied.

"Night!—Tuesday *night!*   And where did you meet him?"

"At the end of Boston pier."

"Ruth! Ruth! alone, and at night!   That was unmaidenly, Ruth!"   His handsome face lost color, and, starting from her, he walked back and forth, struggling with the demon her words had raised.

"You would not blame me if you knew," replied Ruth, gently, yet with a moan in her voice. "I suffer enough," she added, rising as she spoke; "I have enough before me to suffer. Let me go; it is very late. Oh! thank God! I have Him to go to!"

"Ruth!" as he pronounced her name steadily he took her cold, trembling hands in his, and bending forward, gazed as if longing to read a refutation of his doubt in her clear eyes, till they sunk under his look.

"I see nothing like guilt there," he murmured, "and yet —at night—a kiss too. Oh, Ruth! I could almost risk my salvation on your truth to me. I never knew till this moment how absolutely dear you are to me. Don't let me .ove you despairingly, Ruth."

"I can not tell you—not now—perhaps not ever; God knows. You must believe my simple word—I am innocent of any evil intent—of all thoughts of guile."

"Yes, yes, Ruth," he exclaimed, hurriedly; "yes, I believe you—I *do* believe you—I *must* believe you," he added, yet with something of struggling grief and doubt in his words. "But what are they going to do with you in the church?"

"I don't know," she said, slowly, almost losing her self-possession again.

"But you surely will not allow them to inflict—any— punishment on you, Ruth?"

"I have done wrong," she said, meekly.

"A thousand thunders! Wrong! You just told me you were innocent!" cried the Captain, passionately. "Well, my beautiful little batch of sin, confessed and unconfessed, what am I to think of you?" His bantering tone evidently pained her.

"Perhaps it would be better not to think of me at all, Captain Cameron. Perhaps I am not worthy;" her voice broke again a little. "I am poor, dependent, suspected—oh! it would be better for both of us if you never thought of me at all."

"But what if I can't help it?" asked the Captain, vexed at her quiet way (he thought it quiet) of speaking with reference to a love in which his whole soul was bound up. She looked so pure, so perfect in all the faultless contour of her

form and face. He longed to clasp her to his bosom; to tear
her from all adverse influences; to make her his wife. But,
alas! how cold upon his glowing heart fell the shadow her
own assertion had made! The meeting! the kiss at night—
her half-confession.

"Ruth!"

She looked up at him as she was moving toward the door.
He stood there just beside her—a mournful smile adding new
beauty to his splendid face. A dangerous moment was
that!

"Ruth, have you told any one of our engagement?"

She shook her head, blushing a little.

"Come here, my own Ruth," he said, pleadingly, holding
forth his arms; "don't be afraid of me, dear one—none but
God can see us. There! it is very sweet to feel your head
upon my shoulder."

He kissed her upturned brow.

"Ruth, what would you do, if I asked you, for my sake,
to have nothing more to do with the church?"

Starting, as if stung, Ruth tried to free herself from his
arms.

"Stop, Ruth; hear me out. I am a proud man, Ruth—in
spite of my uncertain lineage and the circumstances in which
my childhood was passed, I am very proud. You have told
me of an imprudence—nothing more, I am bound to believe
—committed by you; and you say there is neither guilt or
the shadow of guilt upon your soul. Well, I must, because
I *will*, trust you. In my eyes you are Heaven's holy truth
itself. I know that nothing false has ever passed these lips
—nothing. But those stern churchmen do not know you as
I do. They think you a poor, frail girl—as they pass judgment, I fear, upon all women," he added, bitterly. "It is a
part of their creed to believe everybody evil somewhere, and
it makes them uncharitable to the weak, as they call your
sex. Weak! I wish to Heaven men had your moral strength.
Well, Ruth, a little moment more. If they should do to you
as I have seen them do to others, I fear I should fly to the
uttermost ends of the earth and never come back again. I
couldn't bear it—here I confess my inferiority—my weakness
in contrast to your strength; for I believe that, with the

heroism of an Indian devotee, you would walk on burning
coals, if they commanded. Oh, Ruth! do not let them put
this indignity on *me*—for consider, Ruth, in what relation I
stand to you. Leave them, Ruth, leave them, and go with
me. Let *me* be your religion, Ruth."

She had disengaged herself from his arms, and stood, pale
as death, listening and shuddering. To her awakened consciousness there was an awful presence in that room, over
which the black shadows reeled with every motion of the
bending flame—even the spirit of demonaic darkness. She
felt, as it were, the hot breath of his burning lips, as the
words fell from those of her Captain lover.

"Captain Cameron!"—she paused for a moment, there was
such tumult going on within her—"not even for love such as
yours, would I give up my faith in the visible church. No—
if I am to walk the path of my life alone, suspected and
neglected, so be it—it is my Father's will. If they—the
good, the pure, the tried, think it necessary to my salvation
that I should drink the cup of humility, I am willing, even
to the dregs. Let me go, now, Captain Cameron—I am
dizzy, blind—bewildered—I—"

"Go!" he said, in a voice cold, sharp and clear as a
bell in a winter's night, neither moving nor looking toward
her.

That tone! it fell upon her gentle heart like ice. She
gave one yearning look—she could not help it—no more; but
she said not a word, only turned—slowly, as if it were a pain
to move—groped to the door—opened it—shut it.

Captain Cameron stood there alone, with folded arms.
The light, as the door went to, gave one frantic leap up
toward the darkness, then expired. And the light of that
heart that had steeled itself so—had that, too, gone out?

CHAPTER V.

CAPTAIN BILL IN A NEW CHARACTER.

ALTHOUGH the streets and the taverns were unusually quiet, after a day of so much excitement, there were many private houses from which yet sounded inspiriting music and the mirth of revelry. In the windows of such, the more expensive tapers yet illumined the dimness of a clouded moonlight, while over splendid curtains, shadows of fairy figures could be seen flitting back and forth.

A dark form stood opposite the Governor's mansion. The night was very chill, and he wrapped his cloak closely about him. The naval band sent forth inspiriting strains of old English melodies, and now and then light, laughing voices mingled in. The house stood a little way back from the narrow street. It was built of a grayish stone, and with its deep copings, iron chains that ran from post to post at the doors, heavy moldings on the windows, and massive lion guarding its portals, presented a grand appearance. There was a wide space of garden-land on either side. Great trees, bare of verdure, flung their naked arms up into the cold night. Through the branches flashed innumerable lights—every window was ablaze.

Captain Bill—for the stranger was none other than he—stood silent, as if in deep reflection. Then he walked slowly across the narrow street, and entering the gate, which swung noiselessly open, moved deliberately around the building, making a narrow survey of all the premises, which the strong light enabled him to do.

Through the thin curtains he could see the cook flying from point to point round the great kitchen. The glowing fire, surrounded by smoking dishes, gave indications that a grand supper was in process of preparation, while the savory smell that came through subtle openings made the atmosphere redolent of luxury. The Captain, with much deliberation, watched the hurrying to and fro of the well-fed servants, and muttered to himself:

"That's a goodly turkey he takes from the spit--brown
and juicy. I warrant me the table will be spread with al.
manner of delicacies—plenty of the choicest wines, too.
What's to hinder me from making one of the feast? I've
as good a right. Might count the silver, too—nothing lost.
by being careful. Well, sweet uncle, (looking up to the
parlor windows,) I wish you joy of your reign. I can at
least *smell* your royal dainties. But stop—lean on your oars,
Captain, and reflect. None of this choice company would
know me—save one, possibly two, neither of whom would
dare to expose me. I have it! The dishes are being carried to the table—I'm a wine-merchant, just off the 'Rose'
frigate. I bring news to his Excellency that the Prince of
Orange landed the day—let me see—on the first of last
month; that will do. So, so, I'll get a sup and a taste; see
the goodly company; and, mayhap, my witching little cousin,
Eleanor—taking care to leave my adieus in time to avoid any
particular scene that might possibly occur if it should be as-
certained that my frigate and my occupation are both
fabulous."

While saying this, he had taken from a long, deep pocket
in his cloak, a cocked hat, made of some pliable substance.
Shaping it out decently against his knee, he carried the cap
with the curls attached to the same receptacle, and made
ready to ascend the stone steps. The ponderous knocker
swung to some effect. A servant, in splendid livery of scarlet
and black, came to the door. The gold lacings, cords and
tassels that depended from his gay habiliments flashed out on
the night, and made the opening from the street radiant, like
a view into fairy land. Captain Bill stood there, cocked hat
in hand.

"Can I see his Excellency?" he asked, with cool effront
ery. "I bring important news from England."

The servant, with an obsequious bow, that had followed
the first supercilious glance, ushered him into a private room,
in which, a few moments after, the Governor made his appearance, attended by his secretary. The latter personage
carried himself in a grand way. His manner was affectedly
pompous, and his dress bore the marks of the profuse taste
of a courtier of that courtly period.

The Governor paused in the center of the room, bowed with a stately air, came forward another step, gently moved into its place a massive sword, and bowed again.

"I know not what your Excellency will think of me," said the new-comer, with most consummate coolness and a look of natural embarrassment; "but, in my eagerness to be the first bearer of important news, I came ashore from the frigate 'Rose'—now three miles down the bay—without my documents; nor did I think of that most important mistake until I set foot upon the steps of your residence."

He stood the image of gentlemanly perplexity.

"The frigate 'Rose!' Did we hear aright? And what is thy news, sir?" The Governor's tone was cold, and might have embarrassed an ordinary man.

"The Prince of Orange, your Excellency, landed on the second day of last month, and declared himself king with great state and pomp. On that very day, your Excellency, the frigate 'Rose' dropped out of the Downs, but not before news was sent on board. I should not be here in advance of the frigate, but, with a heavy bribe, I procured the services of one of the sailors, and was boated ashore."

The Governor bowed again—the news seemed not unwelcome.

"To whom," said he, with great gravity, "are we indebted for this information, and why have we not heard the guns announcing the arrival of one of his Majesty's ships-of-the-line?"

"My name, may it please your Excellency, is Brentworth; I am a wine-merchant of London, of the firm of Brentworth and Battersea. I am well aware, your—"

"Mr. Brentworth," said the Governor, smiling graciously, thrown off his guard by the frankness and naturalness of the new-comer, "we are happy to welcome you, sir; your name is a passport anywhere. It is probable that we shall not hear the guns of his Majesty's frigate until morning, when she anchors in the harbor. We beg, Mr. Brentworth, that you will consider yourself our guest to-night. Supper is just being served—we should be happy if you would bear us company to the room where our guests are assembled."

"A thousand thanks," exclaimed the stranger, rising with

a well-acted confusion; "but I am just from the vessel, your Excellency is aware, and the duties of the toilet—"

"Tut! tut!" exclaimed the Governor, smilingly. "We will hear no excuses, and overlook all disarrangement. Thy name is sufficient to cover such minor incongruities, and thine errand motive enough for haste. Andrew, wilt touch the bell? My servant will relieve thee of hat and cloak. And now, sir, this way."

Captain Bill bit his lip, on which lurked the shadow of a sarcastic smile, but seemed nowise daunted, as he followed the Governor into a room blazing with a hundred lusters, pendent from the great English chandeliers, and reflected innumerable times in the long, gilded mirrors.

It was a scene of gay enjoyment upon which he was ushered. The flower of Boston beauty and nobility were congregated there, and the rustling and flashing of heavy brocades, the waving of floating plumes, the lightning-like glitter of precious stones, vied with the radiance of youthful loveliness —the murmur of silvery voices.

For one moment, only one, the adventurous deceiver trembled as he looked—for some of that brilliant company, it was just possible, might know the great wine-merchant, whose reputation was princely in its way. None, however, seemed inclined to dispute his veracity or to claim him as an acquaintance, as is sometimes done by would-know-everybody individuals; and as the news spread, and the élite dallied with it on aristocratic lips, he felt his courage mount, and grew certain that his assurance would carry him over all difficulties.

His boldly-roving eyes followed the imposing pageant until they rested upon two young girls, nieces of the Governor, and cousins, who sat in an alcove, talking with two or three fashionable young men, who, in gay-colored small-clothes of velvet and diamond buckles, stood near them.

Margaret, the elder, pale and elegant, her manner giving evidence of that inimitable repose that marks the high-bred woman, was attired in robes of sparkling blue satin, whose crisp, broad folds fell in a large gleaming circle around her feet. At the entrance of the reputed wine-merchant, the sentence she was forming hung suspended from her lips, and a deadly paleness overspread her face, while her motions became embarrassingly nervous. Her dark eyes and perfectly-molded brow grew troubled, but the excitement that ensued prevented those around her from marking her excessive agitation. Eleanor Saltonstall, her cousin, had one of those faces that always seem looking at you with a laughing menace, however brief may be their glance. Pert, piquant, glowing, versatile in expression, her charming little countenance was now rippled with mock displeasure, anon all geniality and rippling smiles. She was like a marvelous book that, as you read, you wonder what romance is coming next.

Near the two girls stood the Reverend Parris Aldrich, the "Rector," as he was called by his own people. He was the father of Margaret. His parish was exceedingly small, but influential, inasmuch as the Governor was at its head. His wife, a delicate, interesting woman, very much younger than himself, leaned on his arm. The rector wore a look of quiet sadness. His luminous eyes seemed always glancing beyond the object they sought. His head was slightly bald, adding to the expansiveness of a white, broad brow.

At some distance from this group, surrounded by her own circle of admirers, the Lady Anne Bellamont sat, radiant in jewels. She was, perhaps, the only woman of (so-called) noble birth in Boston. No other lady in the room wore ornaments as valuable or garments as rich. Her robes were of exquisitely-lustrous velvet, of a clear ruby color, while on her neck and her splendid arms sparkled every tint of the rainbow. Lady Anne was—nobody knew how near forty; and strangers thought her not many years beyond her teens, so young, fresh and beautiful she contrived to make herself appear. She was admired and feared, for she had a way of saying things both wittily and woundingly. A close observer might have noted that, while Lady Anne Bellamont displayed her dark beauty and keen intellectual powers so lavishly to the multitude, the rector's wife, fragile Mary Aldrich, gazed anxiously toward the bold, handsome vision, and then, with a sigh, drew closer to her husband.

"Uncle Parris," said Eleanor the gay, touching his arm, "something hath disaffected Margaret—she seems ill."

"Margaret, my daughter!" exclaimed the rector, hastily,

and with some alarm in his countenance, as he bent toward her—while her young step-mother hurried to her side, displaying the most affectionate solicitude.

" I feel ill, father—very ill."

Her ghastly face gave evidence of her sickness or perturbation.

" She was well enough before yonder stranger came," said Eleanor, with solicitude in word and manner. "I think she hath taken a spite against the Prince of Orange."

Pale Margaret had arisen, and, leaning on the arm of her father, her mother clasping one of her hands, the three moved toward the door. If news had come from the frigate, where was one who should have brought that news first to her—Sir John Willie, whom the Governor had sent to England on a special mission? A foreboding that some misfortune had happened to him—that was the cause of her paleness.

CHAPTER VI.

THE MIDNIGHT PRISONERS.

MARGARET ALDRICH and her cousin had been sitting together in the drawing-room. Now they had gone out for their embroidery-frames.

There were footsteps sounding in the room again, but not theirs. Some one moved to and fro. The candle was put out with thumb and finger, and the flickering fire-light alone remained to make ghastly images on the walls. Till within a few days, a recess in the room had been appropriated to the use of the Governor's wife, who, with the capricious notions of an invalid, desired to be taken thither. Before this recess, curtains of rich stuff had been hung to keep out the draughts, and they were not yet removed. Now, in the dimness, they rustled strangely, swaying in and out, sending a long swell of chill air toward the embers, which glowed again with momentary brightness.

Then it was quite still.

In a few moments, the cousins entered again. Eleanor, loaded with the huge embroidery-frames, while Margaret carried the candles and a sewing-basket. These latter she placed upon the table—Margaret starting as she exclaimed:

"Did we not leave this candle burning?"

"I thought we did," replied Eleanor, letting fall the frames, that seemed too heavy a burden.

"Strange!" whispered Margaret. "I am certain we did, for I looked back and saw it quite bright and cheerful. Alas! that is but another sign," she added, "and ominous of death."

"Ominous of the wind, rather, I imagine," replied Eleanor, lightly; "as we went from the room the cold air blew it out. The night seems more chill—I will draw the screen up," she added.

They then fell to work, choosing and comparing the bright colors. Up stairs, the Governor dozed, in dressing-gown and easy-chair, while two attendants kept constant watch over the sick lady, sleeping uneasily, and frightened at every motion. For over an hour the young girls plied their pretty task unweariedly, talking softly of many things, while the rustle of the stiff satin under their fingers varied the conversation. At last Eleanor exclaimed:

"There! I have twice broken my silk. I'm tired and sleepy too, I do believe, while your eyes, Margaret, look as sharp as needles. I'm going to lay down—wake me when it nears twelve," and, so saying, she moved to the further end of the room with a languid step, and threw herself, wrapped in a shawl, on one of the couches, her feet toward the recess.

Margaret snuffed the candle—laid by her embroidery-frame also—took from her bosom a locket—looked at it intently, kissed it, then diving into the deep work-basket by her side, drew forth a book.

She sat in a large easy-chair of a crimson color. The dress, of some bright brocade, she wore, well became her stately beauty. She had placed herself before the table—the masses of her dark hair, drawn tightly back by her hands, fell on each side and between the wide draperies of her sleeves in wavy curls. Her elbows rested on the table, her book before her—thus she read, quite absorbed, for nearly another hour.

A shadowy figure, at the end of that time, loomed up gradually from the utmost verge of the room, and, for a moment, stood dimly defined against the somber paneling. Then it made a motion, as of weariness, and the slight form of Eleanor, with its piquant face blanched of its roses, stood before the table in front of the reader.

"Cousin Margaret."

The other gave a frightened start, which sent the book to the opposite end of the table, from thence to the floor.

A laugh, strangely hollow and constrained, burst from the lips of Eleanor Saltonstall.

"Why, coz! did I frighten thee?"

"Indeed thou didst, cousin Eleanor—thou always dost come so silently! Thou art a very shadow, I believe, for motion."

"Something like, since I follow my shadow," replied Eleanor in the same metallic-sounding tones. "Pray, what book is this that is so absorbing?" She stooped and picked it up.

For the first time Margaret looked full in her cousin's face. The look was prolonged to a wondering stare. Why were the cheeks and lips of her merry cousin blanched to a deadly white! Why, although her tones were loud and clear—perhaps louder and clearer than usual—did the muscles of her face quiver as she spoke? Why were the white teeth buried in her lip?

"Ah! I see," said Eleanor, trembling visibly, "a story of castles, of haunted rooms and hobgoblins. Strange taste!—I wonder not I frightened thee. But one need not fear ghosts," she added, with an impressive look at Margaret, who sat wondering if her cousin was growing mad.

"Now, here is a beautiful passage! How fine a description of the ancient castles—the thick ivy creeping to their tower-tops," and, pushing the book before her cousin, the latter saw several lines written in pencil, in an uneven hand, on the broad margin, which, when she made them out, ran thus:

"*There is a man in this room, and, I suspect, armed. He is in the alcove, behind the tapestry. What shall we do? Say something, when you have read this, to prevent suspicion.*"

"A beautiful passage, indeed!" replied Margaret, calmly; but when their eyes met, there was white terror in her face

also. The girls had reason to be alarmed, whether the man
was a burglar or assassin; for the present condition of the
household—sickness, weariness and insubordination of servants,
in a greater or less degree, made such an invasion peculiarly
formidable.

Margaret sat, still pale, but outwardly composed, thinking
as well as her state of bewilderment would allow, while
Eleanor, clasping her little hands tightly, sent imploring
glances toward her elder cousin.

Margaret seized the book again, and wrote, rapidly: "*Be-
have your best.   Go presently to our uncle—I will stay here
alone.   There is no other way.*"

"*It is very late, is it not?*" she asked, in a careless tone, as
Eleanor laid down the book, and seemed quite undecided.

"Yes, hark! the clock says twelve.   Uncle would be angry,
of a certainty, if he knew that we were up at such an hour,"
replied Eleanor.

"Thou wilt go first, then, Eleanor.   I pity thy weary eyes.
I will follow as soon as I have finished this chapter."

Still Eleanor seemed irresolute.   In truth she dreaded to go
through the house by herself, now; especially as her cousin
would be left alone with the intruder.

"I will follow immediately," Margaret repeated, making
rapid gestures for her to go.

Eleanor, taking up a little night-lamp, with a shaking hand,
turned to leave the room.   Her firmness was rapidly deserting
her, while Margaret, though as fully alive to the danger, seemed
to gather strength and courage as the moments passed.   This
she evinced by beginning to sing a light, merry ballad when
the door shut on her cousin, though she kept her glance fastened on the spot where the curtains that hid the object of
their alarm fell moveless.

Not long did this suspense remain, however; for, while she
hummed, listening painfully, all her powers suspended, there
came a quick, sharp rataplan of the grim, lion-headed knocker.
Suppressing a cry of relief, the brave girl sat still, in uncer-
tainty, till she heard the slow steps of the porter, roused
unwillingly from slumber, nearing the hall-door.

Then followed the tread of feet along the passage.   Presently the servant ushered in the Governor's sheriff, and

following him came a face whose recognition almost made her heart stand still.

"Sir John!" she exclaimed—then advanced straight toward him with outstretched hands, while her cheek glowed with some sudden, pleased emotion. The sheriff had glided off, and now sat at some distance, awkwardly crossing his legs and holding his three-cornered hat carefully under his arm.

"I beg you will pardon this unseemly entrance, at such an hour as this—but you will perceive that I am here under arrest;" this he said somewhat haughtily, relinquishing the hand he had held in both of his.

"Under arrest!" exclaimed Margaret, indignantly; "is it possible? Pray, by whose order?"

"By order of the Governor-General, Sir Edmund Andros," he said, bowing low, and almost mockingly. "I was arrested as I came on shore from the frigate 'Rose.'"

Again Margaret's color mounted, and she was so confused and distressed by the various excitements of the hour, that she could say not a word, but stood spellbound before him.

Steps were heard again. The door opened, and appeared, first, the Governor, in his dressing-gown and nightcap, a candle in one hand and a musket in the other. Following his Excellency, came the white, charming face of Eleanor Salton-stall, while making up the rear were three or four servants, sleepy, and looking bewildered and frightened.

The new-comer stepped back for a moment with a glance of scorn.

"Where is this intruder? Halt, sirs! By my halidome! but this seems to be Sir John Willie. Well, sir—so you are the gallant who frightened our fair nieces nearly out of their senses!"

Eleanor whispered to him. Sir John looked on in indignant surprise, as he answered:

"Your Excellency must know that I did not come here of my own good-will. I had the honor of finding your sheriff at my lodgings, waiting for me as I came home from the house of a friend. That, your Excellency, must surely be sufficient apology for my late appearance."

"Very well, sir; very well, sir;" exclaimed the Governor, with choler in both manner and voice. "We will attend to

your case presently.   Meanwhile we offer you the courtesy of
our house.   Be seated, sir."

The gentleman preferred to stand, as he signified by another
haughty bow, and by remaining on his feet.

" Now, men, take your guns to the back of the room and
stand guard—we are four in all, and each able to engage with
a man singly."

" Sir—do you insult me ?" asked the young man, with heat,
thinking these preparations were made on his account.

" By God's mercy !" cried the Governor, " can we not do
our will in our own castle, without being called to account for
it ?   This warlike array hath nothing to do with thee."   The
Governor's voice grew stern as he added, " Concealed by yonder curtain, at the extremity of the room, a villain stands, who
hath entered our domain surreptitiously.   Take aim, men.
Now, fellow ! come forth and lay down your arms or be shot
like a dog."

An awful silence !   Sir John Willie had stepped back, looking with fixed eyes and puzzled brow on the Governor.   The
sheriff gazed on the scene quite terrified.   Margaret, white as
death, pressed her clenched hands to her bosom.   Eleanor
cowered against the wall, holding her hands over her eyes,
while the servants, thus adjured, presented arms, ready for the
word of command.

" When we count three," said the Governor, in a low voice,
" fire !—If our niece was mistaken, there will be but the need
of a little repairing in the arras.   If there be an assassin concealed there, his blood be upon his own head."

" Uncle, uncle, the noise will kill aunt," said Eleanor, in a
hoarse whisper.

" Silence, niece—there will be no need for me to fire," replied the Governor, aside, to her.

" Now, men—one—two—"

Just as the fatal word was about to be pronounced, an
impatient movement was heard.   A hand pressed aside the
curtains, and Captain Bill came defiantly forth, throwing his
weapons upon the lounge.

Margaret, as she saw him, gave a low cry of terror, and fell,
fainting, upon her seat.

" Eleanor, attend to thy cousin," said the Governor; " we

, id thought her of better mettle than to faint at such a time as this. Well, knave "—going forward, he recognized the man by whom he had been so grossly deceived. His countenance changed to a fierce, red wrath.

" So! by God's mercy! this is our wine-merchant come back again! Well, knave—thou *shalt* room with us to-night, whether or no. Thy insolence shall be dearly paid for, I can tell thee. What was the motive to-night, fellow—theft or murder? Confess, or we may give thee a taste of powder yet.'

The man frowned, drew up his tall form, and was silent.

" Sullen, ha!—very well; we'll lodge thee to-night, for sake of the satisfaction of feeling safe with thee under our roof. 'Tis not worth while to call our guards from the fort for such small game. Mr. sheriff, we will see thee early to-morrow. Meantime, Sir John, we consider you a prisoner; you will, therefore, remain here to-night. Men, carry this fellow to the tower-room, at the top of the house," he added, pointing to Captain Bill, " and if he makes the least resistance, shoot him down."

Captain Bill was accordingly escorted to his lodgings, while the Governor remained with Sir John Willie. Margaret had been led, long before, to her chamber.

Sir John Willie had been a free citizen of America for some twelve years. On his coming to the colonies, he had immediately invested his money in cloths, and through good business talents had amassed a considerable fortune. He had paid his addresses formally to Margaret Aldrich; but as rector Aldrich, her father, had given her in ward to his brother-in-law, the Governor, that gentleman had taken a very great interest in his niece, and had presumed to dictate in the matter.

Sir John, being in politics (though somewhat secretly so) what would be called a democrat at the present day, the Governor was very angry at his presumption in wishing to marry his niece, saying further that he had not looked for her to wed a petty trader, as he designated Sir John. So he laid every hindrance in the way, and finally gave him a commission to England which would occupy some three years, and that time had now expired.

Sir John Willie—who never wished any one to address him

by his prefix, was a prodigious favorite with the people of Boston. He had written two books which were printed in Cambridge, and were greedily read. His embarkation for England was quite a little triumph, and at his return no less an ovation was offered him, especially as it was well known that he brought news of importance to the Colonies, the publication of which, before it reached the Governor in writing, gave that dignitary great offense.

The Governor, as his nieces left the drawing-room, strode up and down several times, apparently very impatient with his own hot temper, or else at the calmness of Sir John. The latter was of a very slight figure, while his Excellence inclined to be portly. Both were fine-looking men, although the silken nightcap, with its dangling tassel hopping and bobbing about the Governor's nose as he walked with inclined head, made him appear a little ludicrous.

Presently he stopped, and in a voice intended to be calm, yet which was very imperious, he put several questions to Sir John, all of which were quietly and respectfully answered.

" I understand you caused this declaration of the Prince of Orange to be printed in order that the *people* might get it first," he said at last, with some heat.

" I certainly did get it printed for the people," said Sir John, " but I am not aware that I had any choice as to its first disposition. I would as soon you had seen it as they."

" As soon ! as soon !" cried the Governor ; " by God's mercy ! do we hear aright ? Thou hadst *as soon* I had obtained the document as the people ?"

" Why not, your Excellency ?"

" Why not ? Are we to be classed with the commonalty? With shopkeepers, with cartwrights, with tailors, with trip-hammer mountebanks ? As soon ! forsooth ! Pray, dost thou put thyself on a level with us ?"

" I am aware that the office of your Excellency should be esteemed of much account. I am also as well aware, *vox populi vox dei.*"

" We do not want thy Latin scraps," exclaimed the Governor, passionately ; " we wish to know why your knightship did not first bring *us* the news of the royal proclamation ?"

"I was not aware, your Excellency, that it was customary for passengers to do so," said Sir John, commanding his voice and temper; "neither did I ever hear it was any man's duty so to do, unless he felt inclined."

"By God's mercy!" cried the Governor, "but thou art impertinent, sir."

"It was not my intention, Excellency," Sir John dispassionately answered.

"We command thee to give into our hands the declaration of which we have heard," cried the chief magistrate, in fury.

"I decline to do so, Excellency," was the still calm reply.

"Sir, thou art a saucy fellow—a scurvy fellow—a God-forsaken fellow! We will see if we are to be treated with contempt by a clothier. Sir, thou art a knave—a blockhead—a disgrace to thy country!" and the Governor strode to and fro in his wrath.

"Excellency, you are the Governor; that title covers all defects!" Sir John provokingly added, with a look which showed how his soul burned within him.

"By God's mercy! if our guard were here thou shouldst be carried into the fort and dieted. Thou art crazy, thou loon! To-morrow we will send thee before the magistrate. We will see what can be done, *sub colore juris.*"

Sir John was not disconcerted. He answered: "Your Excellency may call this right, but remember that, *summum jus, summa injuria.*"

"We will see—we will see who and what has the right. *As soon*—by God's mercy! the fellow hath put contempt upon us." The Governor almost wept in his rage.

"Perhaps, your Excellency, the townsmen may see this matter in *my* light," he said, still maintaining his provoking composure.

"And what care I," fairly roared the Governor, "for the *townsmen!* Are they not my subjects by virtue of his Majesty? Let them open their mouths about it if they dare! I'll gag them with taxes."

"Governors are but flesh and blood," replied the calm Sir John.

"By God's mercy! force me not to extremities. I have told thee once, thou shalt have the courtesy of my house so

far as food, lodging and shelter go," exclaimed the Governor,
irritated beyond measure, and yet feeling that he had acted in
a manner unbecoming his dignity.   "My servants, some of
them, will show thee a chamber;" so saying he pulled a cord
near him, and a sleepy porter soon appearing, the room was
left deserted.

CHAPTER VII.

THE THIEF ESCAPED.

SIR JOHN WILLIE, by order of the Governor, breakfasted
in a room apart, the next morning.   His Excellency, with his
two nieces, sat at their own table, and were languidly sipping
coffee when a servant-girl entered, white with dismay, and
following her the stately body of Mrs. Martha Clough, the
housekeeper—a genial English woman, her broad cap-ribbons
flying back over her thick shoulders.

"Oh ! sir, if you please, the great silver vase is gone, and
all the spoons, and some of the best linens and tankards, and
the creamer and sugar, and the Lord knows what all," she
cried, wringing her hands.

"I hope your Excellency won't blame me nor *h*any of the
servants," put in the tall, broad housekeeper.   "With these
here very keys—as I were very prompt to do since I were
with your Excellency—with these very keys I locked up
*h*every thing, and now I find that *h*all is gone, savin' and
exceptin' which were put up 'ere in the 'all and closet.
There is been thieves in this 'ouse, your Excellency."

The Governor was astounded ; Margaret trembled like a
leaf as she cried, with a terrible agitation in her voice, "Why,
Clough ! *who* could have done it ?"

Instant search was made, however, and other pieces of
plate were missing.   Where was the thief, and who ?   The
house had been thoroughly searched on the previous night.
Of course every one thought of the prisoner up-stairs.   The
porter was sent for and smartly interrogated.   He left the
man asleep, he said—that is, he thought so, hearing no noise,

and supposed the Governor did not want the door opened till the proper authorities were present.

"There they come now," responded the Governor, a loud official rap sounding.

The sheriff, who had ushered in Sir John Willie, the night before, accompanied by a brother officer, entered, and the Governor briefly related the circumstances.

"We left him secure enough, your Excellency," said the pompous little sheriff, a man short even to dumpiness, his hair a touchy red, and curled so tightly that it looked one huge knot. "Did your Excellency take charge of his weapons?"

"Yes, they are—by God's mercy! we placed them here on this mantel last night, behind the chandeliers," he cried, perceiving that the shelf was quite empty. Then turning, he inspected the place from which the weapons had vanished.

"There seemeth to be a paper rammed in this opening," he said, pointing to a crevice in the paneling. "Margaret, thy fingers are smaller than mine; try if thou canst dislodge it."

Margaret came forward. All eyes were fixed upon her, for the rigidity of her muscles, in her efforts to appear self-composed, and the extreme pallor of her usually pale countenance, were obviously marked. For a moment she worked at the paper—it loosened and came out—and upon unfolding it, were these reckless words written in pencil:

"*Tell the Governor he may go to grass, is the message of*
"CAPTAIN BILL."

"That cursed pirate Captain!" exclaimed the sheriff; "for two years we have tried to bring him to justice."

Governor Andros turned pale with passion. "By God's mercy!" he cried, "did we cage that villain? We had him safe enough the last night, locked in, bolted and guarded. There is some conspiracy going on in this house, and yet I'd as soon suspect myself as my trusty valets. They have been with me from childhood."

The porter was summoned.

"Lead to the prison-room," said the Governor.

The man obeyed with trembling. "Things looked mighty mysterus," as he had declared to the servants.

"Its woudrously still here," said the sheriff, as they gained the top and glanced at the musty walls, where, in the coruers, hung the blurred webs of octogenarian spiders.

The porter, declaring that the key had not been out of his hauds for a single momeut, turned it in the lock, remarking, as he did so, "They do say that some of these wicked people do have familiars to help 'em off, sir— and I don't doubt it be so, for—"

"Unbolt the door!" said the Governor.

."Nobody here! This is outrageous! This is damnable! By God's merey, I will find out the knave who hath doue this. Twice hath this fellow escaped us. John," he coutinued, turuing sternly to the porter, "I hold you accountable for this man's escape."

"Oh! your Honor! Oh! your Excelleney!" cried the poor porter, falling on his knees, his white face terror-stamped— "Oh, good master! for Dolly's sake—for my own good, sweet reputation, don't suspect me, sir—me, who has grown up with your Excelleney, and was the son of your father's porter. I did my duty—I didn't close my eyes all the blessed night; and if he went, he weut by the devil. I do assure your worship that there was a smell of brimstone here this moruing—"

"Get up!" cried the Governor, cutting short his harangue— "Into the chamber, varlet. I shall lock thee up, and then if thou wilt escape by the same means, we will throw away all suspicion of thy intent, and thou shalt hereafter be placed in a gilded box, to be labeled and carried about the streets, to show meu what good service the devil doeth to those who serve him."

"Oh! good master! Oh! merciful Excellency—" but the door was shut on his pleading.

While the Governor was giving directions concerning Sir John Willie to the little sheriff, his secretary entered—bringing in a sweet perfume, that exhaled from his dainty locks, and his embroidered kerchief.

His sword and chains rattled as he walked, and his immaculate shirt-frills, uewly starched, glistened iu advance of him.

The Governor greeted him, waiting impatiently for what he had to say.

"Your Excelleucy will be astouished to hear," he began,

with a flourish intended for a bow, " that the knave of whom
I demanded the church-key in your Excellency's name, did
refuse it with sundry impertinent speeches, and also that your
humble servant was openly insulted through one master Cameron, beggarly Captain of a small ship which hath laid out in
the harbor for the space of two months. The said master did
pour out vile detraction upon the name of your Excellency,
setting at defiance the threats of your humble servant, and
laughing to scorn your Excellency's government, calling it
tyranny, and sundry obnoxious names."

" By God's mercy !" exclaimed the Governor, in low, fierce
tones, " what manner of people have we to reign over ? Why
didst thou not immediately put this saucy knave under arrest ?"

" I sent men as soon as possible after him, your Excellency,
and spent the greater part of the night in vain attempts to
bring him to justice. Even now the officers are on his track,
and I hope soon to inform your Excellency that he is safe in
the common jail ;" so making a very a low and courtly bow,
he stood upright, while the Governor, with knit brows and eyes
bent on the floor at his feet, muttered, " That maketh two varlets we will have to justice. By God's mercy, but we will
subdue this rebellious people."

CHAPTER VIII.

COTTON MATHER'S DRAMA.

THE church of the Mathers could boast of but little archi-
tectural beauty. Its material was of wood, and it stood
squarely and sturdily upon a mossy lawn. No sculpture
relieved its rude portals, nor stained glass let in the many-col-
ored rays. Trees, whose roots were untwined from the mold
for the planting of this old oak of Christ, let their leaves softly
in between the hot light of day and the quiet somberness of
the sanctuary. Its steeple was square and devoid of all pre-
tension to elegance ; but the true-tongued bell, that hung up in
its tower, often

> "Swung out and swung loud,
> Telling to the village crowd,
> Standing by the open grave,
> God recalled but what he gave;
> Sung, swinging free and wide,
> Joyous pæans for the bride;
> Called, from their dwellings lowly,
> Maidens fair and old men holy."

The choir-gallery, with its broad, brown molding, was
placed opposite the pulpit.   No damask curtains concealed
the rosy faces of the choristers.   There, what triumphs did
father Comstock achieve with the ungodly bass-fiddle, which
some of the over-strict but good and conscientious deacons
were " very much set against."

Gloriously sounded kingly " Old Hundred," and noble
" Corinth," airs made sacred by the heart-worship of a century.

On the Sabbath morning of which we write, the few singers
assembled slowly, and with downcast faces, in their accustomed seats.   Father Comstock, chorister, met them all without his usual smile.   The old man's " specs " seemed dim,
for he took them down to wipe them oftener than was his
wont, and it was noticed that he frequently gazed at the place
where Ruth's sweet face had always before met him—for Ruth
was head-singer in the church of the Mathers.

" Who's to take Miss Margerie's place to-day ?" asked a
broad-faced, cherry-cheeked girl, thoughtlessly.

" Nobody !"

The old man had turned to her as if stung, and his mouth
opened and shut mechanically, as he repeated, in a sharp, curt
tone, " Nobody !"   So there stood her empty seat, and there
laid her book, with the narrow blue mark hanging from
between its leaves as she had last used it.   And when some
one came in and would have appropriated it, the old man
without a word, laid his yellow, sinewy hand tenderly upon
it, and gave his own book to the stranger.

It was nearing the time for service.   Now and then some
bent and aged body crept down the alley and into the humble
pew.   In fact, they were all humble.   Only the morning sun
laid its crimson over their backs.   The pauper who hobbled
from the near " work'us " knew that his hobnailed shoes
rested on no softer surface than those of the well-to-do merchant at his elbow.

Above, the trunks of trees, but rudely squared, crossed their huge beams, and roughly folded in their massive grasp the walls that years had not yet worn gray. The windows, very high, and set in deep embrasures, seemed dim for the loss of dear forms that could gather no more light from them, save when the red day let golden arrows on their graves.

Over the pulpit swung the old sounding-board, that gave the thunder of the voice-denunciatory a far-sounding echo. Under that, the right hand struck the strong desk, and thumped the board-covered Bible, giving emphasis to truth.

Without was the hush of the Pilgrim Sabbath. A little twittering bird-music, such as we often hear when the ground is white and the snow-bells ringing, sounded among the leafless branches, and river and vale gathered together their precious incense and offered it up to God. From dwellings, far and near, came all who were able to leave their homes; and as, on extraordinary occasions, a church is always full, so, perhaps, a few rheumatics found it possible to limp out, and here and there a feeble sister kept up her strength and spirits along the road by anticipation.

Sometimes they came in twos from a distance, the good-wife on a pillow behind her husband, and as they dismounted and tied the old horse where he could leisurely browse, they made a brave show. Generally those who rode were of the wealthier class, and wore golden buckles, flowing wig, shining knee-bands and the costliest of cocked hats, while the goodwife displayed a silken gown, trimmed with modest ruffles, and sported enormous bows on her deep bonnet. Entering, the women and girls filed off to their seats, while in an opposite direction the men and boys established themselves, both sexes looking so demurely down that one would have thought they feared a smile as they did a pestilence.

The minister was a man of too much stateliness and consequence to enter the same door with the people. When, therefore, he came in, near his pulpit, escorted by the sexton, every face looked in expectation to see Ruth. It was with a shrinking, grieved glance with most, especially the elder part of the congregation. In some of the youthful, curiosity was not unmixed with satisfaction. Their more common minds had not comprehended the beauty of her character, and hence

they were not sorry to see the universal favorite and moral
pattern humbled.

The minister's wife came in—and there, too, came Ruth.
Poor, pale Ruth! sustaining herself with difficulty, so much did
the long, flowing black garment impede her movements.
Slowly — and, oh! so white! so bowed! so utterly over-
whelmed!

Her face, in contrast to the dead black of her garment,
seemed like marble of the purest, clearest luster. No trace of
color—almost no trace of life. Never once were the blue eyes
lifted—the long lashes seemed as if glued to the cheek. With
folded hands upon her bosom, and glittering, wavy hair, flowing, in token of humiliation—so wo-begone she looked, and
yet so saintly, that, as she moved along the alley to take the
position of the penitent, sobs sounded all over the house.
White-headed men bent low over their staffs; children won-
dered and grieved—tears rolled down the cheeks of maidens,
and old father Comstock sat, all gathered in a shrinking heap,
his face buried in his hands, and trembling from head to foot
with his sorrow and his sympathy.

But when Ruth had gained her stopping-place and turned
toward the pulpit, half her anguish was gone. It must have
been that some supporting angel had an arm beneath her, for
now the sweet features seemed as calm, even as firm as sculp-
tured marble—the eyes were nearly closed, and a light, as from
heaven, appeared to glorify her face and her fair, shining hair.
Her hands were raised a little and tightly locked together, as
if in supplication.

Perhaps when the psalm was sung, especially the verse—

> "Lo! I am treated like a worm,
> Like none of human birth,
> Not only by the great reviled,
> But made the rabble's mirth,"

her head sunk a little lower, and there was a shining circle
around the bright edges of her lashes, but it was only for a
moment. She had borne the heaviest of the cross—she was
resting now—while, for her sorrow, even the great bass-viol,
touched by trembling fingers, seemed to sob and groan. Rev-
erent as were the people on their Pilgrim Sabbaths, there never
was such a hush—such a palpable, spirit-awed silence, as on

that occasion, especially the second preceding the opening of the paper, Ruth's confession, which Cotton Mather held in his hands with all due seriousness.

At that moment the young ship-master entered ; noiselessly and almost unobserved, he glided to a seat near where Ruth stood. There was lightning in the eyes that glanced with such defiance in their sweep around the congregation. There was a nameless something, a terrible expectancy, resting on those firm, beautiful features. The hair was tossed angrily back. The broad chest rose and fell, and swelled like the waves of the sea in a great storm. The lips were not set, but *clenched* together, and the right hand worked convulsively.

In a loud and sonorous tone the minister began :

" I, Ruth Margerie, do hereby, in ye presence of Almighty God and ye people here assembled, declare and make my confession unto this church, that I took part in a profane play, thereby bringing scandal on ye church of Christ. Alsoe, I did—"

" Hold !" cried a voice, whose tone sent thrills through every heart in the assembly. It startled Ruth out of all composure. Her pale cheek flushed, and she glanced from right to left, frightened and trembling. The minister paused—rested both hands on the pulpit that he might speak with the energy needed for the occasion—but, quicker than thought, the young ship-master started from the place where he stood, almost shaking with the tumult of his soul—gained Ruth's side, laid one hand firmly on her shoulder, with a dextrous movement unwound the odious garment from her person, and, gathering it up in his hands, said wildly, as he hurled it down the middle alley :

" I fling the lie into the teeth of this church, as I fling the garment of your miserable superstition to the ground. Who *dare* accuse Ruth Margerie of wrong ?"

The whole congregation had sprung, as one man, to their feet. Some looked up to see if instant thunderbolts would not descend to smite the profane wretch. Cotton Mather seemed like one petrified—the flame of outraged sacredness hot-leaping from his heart.

Ruth herself, with a low moan, had sunk to her knees, and was weeping tears of fright and grief.

" Wretched, perfidious young person !" shouted Cotton Mather, lifting his arm ; " Knowest thou not that the vengeance
of God will fall upon thine accursed head for this daring des-
ecration in these courts of the Lord's house ?—for this insult to
his ministering servant ? Maiden, I do command thee, take
up the garb of thy humility, and clothe thyself in it with all
humility."

" She shall not !" cried the ship-master ; " I have sworn it,"
and lifting Ruth, now nearly unconscious, in his strong arms,
he bore her rapidly from the house, loosened the bridle of his
horse, and springing on the saddle with his burden, rode
straight to the door of Mistress Bean, and, while the good
woman shrunk from him with horror, told the deed he had
performed.

" But, mayhap, you've done a greater harm to the maid in
the eyes of the people," she said, her voice unwontedly stern.
He had not thought of that. The delirium of his passion—
in truth it was partly directed toward Ruth herself—was softening down. He hurried from the house, leaped in the saddle again—and was arrested long before the sun had gone
down, though not till after a desperate resistance. So it happened that another inmate was added to those already in the
gloomy jail.

<hr />

CHAPTER IX.

VIEWS FROM A CLOSET.

As full of curious importance as a nut is full of meat, Gaffer Scates popped about from street to street, speaking to this
one, nodding to that, with odd winkings, blinkings and shoul-
der-shruggings. Now he would stop a staid, sedate, puritanic
old gentleman, whisper a word and begone, then take by the
button some dapper free-and-easy politician, give him a word
and a wink, chuckle, and whiz off like a cannon-ball that
knows just where to go.

Plainly speaking, the respectable little city of Boston was
in a hubbub. Up the steep hills and round the winding lanes

—at the sign of the "Blue Dog and Rainbow," "Dog and Pot," "Cabinet and Drawers," "King's Arms"—in all the alleys—at all the grocers', haberdashers', linen-drapers', etc., etc., men, women and children were talking, talking, talking.

A murder!—such a shocking murder!—right in the harbor! —close under the walls of their very homes! And a sight it was to see the poor things, covered with bloody flags, carried up Hanover street—over the swing-bridge—down Prison lane —a great rabble after them, moving noiselessly along in the direction of the fort, where the bodies were finally deposited.

As usual in such cases, there were all sorts of rumors afloat. Some said that the young Captain, Cameron, had freed himself, and determining to get possession of his vessel, had gone out and killed the soldiers—they not reflecting that it would be rather difficult to start a ship to sea without a crew. Others declared that the terrible "Red Hand" and other pirates were right in their midst, and that life and property were no longer secure.

"Red Hand!" exclaimed a shrunken old man, very slow and infirm of speech, standing in the midst of a knot of women, who, in their blue short-gowns, red petticoats, high shoes and snowy caps, made a picturesque group. "I remember me, only thirty years agone he was the finest little lad I ever set my two een on. He's a young man yet, and capable of a master 'mount of mischief if they don't take him."

"Ay!" remarked a woman, "and Faith Justin was a prettie lassie when he married her. Her cheeks were red as roses, and her eyes as bright as diamonds. Poor young thing! She's been dead now—how many years, neighbor?"

"Something like ten, I should say, mistress," was the reply.

"Well, it's better she didn't live and get her heart broken. I'm sure the poor child she's left—"

The noisy blast of a trumpet drowned the speaker's voice. A single horseman came galloping down the street. He sat a noble steed, whose gay caparisons, prancing and curvetings, together with the brilliant red uniform of his rider, commanded general attention and admiration. At every window, young and old flocked to see and listen.

"God save the king!

"Hear ye! hear ye!" shouted the man, for a moment reining in his superb horse.

"The Governor proclaimeth that the service of the Church of England, the true and lawful worship of a people, will be performed· in the South church, God willing, on the next Sabbath morning, at ten o'clock of the day. All true and loyal subjects of his Majesty will accordingly meet at the time and place appointed. Hear ye! hear ye!"

A blast and flourish of the trumpet, loud and long—the handsome horse pranced proudly on, and soon, in a more distant direction, the stentorian voice was heard, crying, "God save the king!"

"Now, is not that too much for flesh and blood to bear?" asked Gaffer Scates, with purple-red face. "Three times have our people refused the key of our church; twice have committees waited upon his Excellency, and yet after this infinite fuss and pains, he taketh the matter out of our hands, by proclaiming, by this spurred courier, that he is lord and master, and the thing *shall* be done. Can flesh and blood stand so much?"

It was yet very early, and the morning was one of unusual loveliness. Blue and brilliant the royal sky arched with the bend of a conqueror over the world, and the sun hung banners wherever he smiled. From the country, down the hilly, winding roads, came the loaded market-wagons. The air seemed almost as bland as the breath of summer, yet men appeared not to note how beautiful it was. Only careful women opened wide their windows and hung out their household stuffs to be purified, and the tender laugh of babes, who had been long housed, floated out to the passers-by. Men met together in their places of business, not to talk of stocks or the weather, but their faces were anxious, and their voices suppressed. Ofttimes through the day, the Governor's secretary rode through the streets, in his haughty, defiant manner; but wherever he was seen, execrations were liberally bestowed upon him and the obnoxious power he served. His name was coupled with those of Jeffries and Colonel Percy Kirke, monsters of cruelty and treachery, whose like could hardly be paralleled in centuries. But had he the power, said the people, he would prove to be just such another

They fully (and rightly) believed him their enemy in every thing, and if they had not, his overbearing and insolent demeanor, his contemptuous declarations toward tradespeople, his boastings of the consideration with which he had been treated by the king, and even of amours and intrigues which were a shame to decency, had made him an object of suspision and even of hatred.

It was plainly to be seen that he held the mind of the Governor in his grasp, and partially molded it to his will. Notwithstanding his foppish love of dress, and his arbitrary assumption of dignity—with which he was wont to puff and swell like the fabled frog—he possessed the consummate art of the tactician. Seizing the opportunity at just the right moment of time, he managed so as always to secure the Governor's hearing, and placed his reasoning in such a light as to make it seem the result of the thoughts and plannings of all the wisest heads in the Colony.

So, in different directions, this suspicious officer and Gaffer Scates spent the day, apparently in electioneering for their separate purposes.

Meanwhile, Mistress Bean was engaged to get up a plain supper at the Red Lion. It was not an unusual thing to prepare feasts and collations, but on this day every thing seemed to go wrong with Mistress Bean. In truth, she felt uneasy on Ruth's account. By cold looks and cold speeches she had driven her away, and Ruth's quiet smile had, unconsciously to her, become indispensable. The house seemed colder, the maids crosser, the fires burned more faint, the viands did not suit—for Ruth, upon such occasions, had always been chief taster, and according to her judgment the spices and other condiments were mixed. So the hostess sent for Mistress Comstock, and the two worked and worried together.

The supper was to be laid at nine, in the dining-hall, and previous to that the company were assembled in the large back parlor, the front parlor having been secured, as Mistress Bean said, by letter, for a select number of gentlemen who were to be engaged in some town business. At eight o'clock both rooms were occupied. In the front parlor were the Governor's secretary, Doctor Bullivant and other gentlemen. They had but one light, and that burnt dimly, apparently by

design.   At the end of the room adjoining the back parlor
was a closet that had doors opening into both rooms.   The
upper half of these doors was of glass, shaded, but not concealed, by curtains of thin muslin.   From the closet came
one of the gentlemen, saying, in an excited way:

"They seem to be all assembled now, and are beginning
their talk.   We can hear very plainly in the closet, two of
the panes being broken near the top of the door."

"Let us go in, then," said the secretary; whereupon the
rest hastily arose and stationed themselves in the closet.

From that position might be seen a score of men seated
about the great round table, and on chairs at the sides of the
room.   Hanging from the walls, or perched on convenient
places, were cocked hats, canes and overcoats.   Upon the center of the table lay the great Bible, bound in boards and
clasped with iron.   Conspicuous among the gentlemen was
Doctor Cotton Mather, who had just read a chapter.   Beside
him sat Master Gamaliel Whiting, straight as if glued to his
tall chair-back, whose Gothic points sprung far above his
head.   His knees were crossed, and the silver buckles on his
shoes sparkled in the fire-light.

The high-handed outrages of the Governor had inflamed
the whole Colony, as the conversation of the assembled worthies will show.   Father Comstock and Scates, prominent
townsmen, Cotton Mather and the schoolmaster Whiting
were gathered in the huge sitting-room of the Red Lion tavern.   Sitting far apart was Captain Cameron's servant, Marmaduke Catchcod, who was even then under arrest for using
seditious language.   He could not or would not remember to
call the Governor "his Excellency," but feigned to forget, and
used all manner of comical titles.   In the little closet, where
the Governor's secretary had hidden himself with Doctor Bullivant, he could hear all that was said.

Father Comstock and Gaffer Scates sat side by side, and
the rest of the company was composed of eminent merchants
and townsmen of Boston.

The conversation, sustained at first by a few, began to grow
more general.   The clear sound of Mather's abrupt and for
cible English, taking precedence of all the rest, rung with a
more sonorous tone than usual.

"It is hard, brethren, to see our dearly-bought privileges wrested from us thus, by the hand of an unscrupulous tyrant, whom the king hath sent to look out for our interest; but, nevertheless, God knoweth, and judgeth also," he added, with strong emphasis.

"Is not that treason?" muttered the secretary.

"He looketh out little for your interests, methinks, brother Mather," said the schoolmaster; "I should say he thinketh little for any interest save his own."

"Truly!" cried father Comstock; "and 'tis said he intend eth to make a new law concerning marriages—that no contract of that kind be considered valid, save it be solemnized by a minister of the Church of England. A pretty pack of heathens he would make of us. To think that I should wake up some morning and find that Mistress Comstock and I had been living in sin for forty years of our lives!"

"And I hear, for the probate of merchant Dudley's will, he hath caused forty shillings to be exacted," said Gaffer Scates.

"Is there no way to be rid of such abominable taxation?" asked schoolmaster Whiting.

"What are we to do?" exclaimed another. "He hath caused us to be deprived of our charter; he hath misrepresented us to the king; he hath abused his power and our confidence in many direct ways; he hath drawn his allies and parasites around him to keep him in countenance and gag us. Thou seest he has sorely crippled us, Master Whiting."

"Thou canst tell me no new thing of Sir Edmund Andros," responded the schoolmaster, speaking with his usual deliberation. "I have not yet forgotten his marching into Hartford, within these few months, with his sixty troops, and the time we had to lodge and victual them. I do believe it took all the provender of our poor little town, so that it hath not been so favorable in that way since. One would have thought our Governor might have moved a stony heart, laboring to tell, almost with tears, how that we had been to so great and sad expense in planting our little Colony. Thou shouldst have heard him that day."

"Master Whiting, thy hand again!" cried old father Comstock, with enthusiasm. "Didst thou verily hear and see the whole?" The old man trembled with excitement.

"I truly saw all that could be seen, for thou knowest there came a short period of darkness."

"How did our roaring lion of a Governor listen?" asked Cotton Mather.

"Roaring lion!" hissed the secretary, in his dark closet, shaking with sudden rage. "Hear it! Hast thy book with thee? Pencil it down; pencil it down, doctor. Roaring lion! ha!"

"He listened with the petty pompousness which he ever affecteth," replied the schoolmaster; "but he hath a hard heart. Sitting in his splendid uniform, his whelp beside him —['Oh! the pestilent knave!' cried the secretary, grinding his teeth; 'that's me. Book it, doctor, book it!']—taking minutes, his officers glittering in red and gold, his guard of halberts and musketeers standing a short way off—he made answer with most insolent coolness, that all this eloquence was wasted on him—['Verily was it!' muttered Mather]— that he bore the king's commands, and must execute his Majesty's orders. At this I observed that whelp of his to chuckle."

"That's me again—book it, doctor, book it!" cried the secretary between his teeth, and pressing the shoulder of his friend heavily.

"He may chuckle on the wrong side of his mouth yet," said Gaffer Seates, with valiant emphasis.

With constant reiterations to "Book it, doctor, book it," the secretary listened, his wrath increasing, and muttering ever and anon, "Why doth not that hound of a sheriff come?"

"At length," resumed the schoolmaster, "evening came. The lights were placed upon the table, and the debate still went on, Sir Edmund never giving in an inch. I was there with ten of my lads, from fourteen to seventeen, (my Latin class,) they being impetuously angry at the doings, and wishing to rush in pell-mell, when the charter was brought; but that I would not allow. Our townsmen had assembled in great numbers, and one of them, a Master Wadsworth, commander of the 'Phœnix,' a goodly ship, stood near the Governor, and I did notice, once or twice, an expressive glance between the two. I confess I trembled for our poor charter, and would fain have snatched it from such power; but suddenly there fell a great darkness—every candle was put out. Never was I in such a solemn quiet as followed. Only the Governor-General, after a moment, cried out, 'By God's mercy!' and there was a rattle of muskets by the guards.

"'Light!' cried the Governor; and before the word had quite passed his lips, the candles were burning, and every man looked at his neighbor with an innocent amazement.

"But the charter was nowhere to be seen!"

A tear glittered through the smile in his eye, when, as the schoolmaster said this, every hand, as if by one impulse, came heavily down upon the table.

"My lads cried like babies," continued the schoolmaster, "and I'm not sure but older eyes grew moistened. There was a subdued joy—a mute, huzza-like glance went from man to man. There was no need of shouts—the deed itself was a shout that has not been silenced to this day. Where the charter is, we know not; nor shall we know till this scourge be taken from New England."

"This scourge! book that, doctor!" cried the secretary, growing every moment more furious. "Oh! what a precious case we'll make for these rebels!"

"Well say'st thou scourge, schoolmaster," exclaimed Cotton Mather; "he hath been indeed a scourge unto us, 'specially unto *our* family—tormentor of my father and myself in divers ways. On the Sabbath he takes our meeting-house for his Papistical ceremonies, for, like his master, we know he inclineth to the Romans. It is an outrage such as a people might feel justified in resenting, yet I tell my charge to quietly submit, for the great God will appear for us. These various imprisonments, taxations and tyrannies shall be fearfully accounted for, as I am a minister of the Word. For truly that man hath been a curse to this country since he first set foot on our soil. And of his secretary—I do hereby declare him to be a blasted wretch, who shall die forsaken of God and man!"

The secretary, at this, was in such a tumult of rage that he nearly choked, and tore at his throat, gasping; then, half drawing his sword, he would have rushed in upon the company, but the doctor prevented him.

" And now, friends," said Cotton Mather, reaching for his hat, " I must begone. I would stay to tne supper, but busi- ness calls, and Mr. Ross will be in waiting for me."

" Stop him! oh! for one minute," groaned the Governor's minion. " The sheriff must be here even now, I am certain —that is his step."

" I meant to talk over touching the affair of Sir John Wil- lie, but I leave the matter to thy discussion," added Cotton Mather, quietly. " I would only advise that, for *the present* ye bear with the ills which may shortly be put a stop to by the people of—"

" Treason!" cried a smothered voice.

" We have listeners here," said the minister.

The closet door burst open and the secretary appeared, with features convulsed and clothes disarranged. He sprung to- ward Cotton Mather, who, with calm dignity, kept his ground, while the company arose to protect him.

" You called me a whelp, braggart!" shouted the secretary, flashing his anger upon the statue-like face of the reverend man.

" Yes—I called thee lion's whelp, if I remember aright," said the undaunted Mather. " I beg thy pardon—I used the wrong terms, and, in my version, I denominate thee—whelp and child of Satan."

" Thou foul-mouthed charlatan, dost thou not know that thy contemptible *life* is in my power?" foamed the angry man.

" Thou poor son of perdition!" said Cotton Mather, half pityingly, half contemptuously—" go home to thy chamber, and get on thy knees—and God help thee to repent. Gentle- men—I wish you good evening.

" Stop! I arrest thee!" shouted the secretary.

" Where is thy authority?" asked Cotton Mather, with his cool smile.

" The king! in his name I arrest thee."

" I fling thy authority to the winds!" saying which, with the most provoking blandness, Cotton Mather bowed to the company and left the room.

" Oh! gentlemen! gentlemen!" said Mistress Bean, now making her appearance with Mistress Comstock. " I hope there will be no trouble in my house. Noble sir," (courtesying to the secretary,) " I am honored by thy presence, surely—but I did not think there would be a difficulty. I hope you will let these gentlemen come in to their supper."

" Let them! *let* them !" cried father Comstock, flushing, while, as he lifted himself, Gaffer Scates crept to the further end of the table.

" Ay ! *let* them! She hath the right word, old white-crown —and yonder comes my power to let or no," cried the secretary, choked with his passion. " Lead them all to jail, Mr. sheriff, every mother's son of them—lead them off."

" I demand the reading of the warrant first," said the schoolmaster, facing the red-eyed secretary.

" No warrant shall be read—off with them, I say ; lead off."

" Thou dost exceed thine office, good man," said the master, his eyes beginning to blaze, though their deep depths had been kindling some time.

" Good man ! thou tapeworm ! thou knitting-needle ! Don't *good man me*, or by the heavens—"

" For mercy's sake, gentlemen !" screamed Mistress Bean, as the secretary drew his sword, and the schoolmaster brought from his heavy cane a long, stiletto-like blade. " Oh ! help ! help ! we shall have murder here."

Instant confusion reigned. The gentlemen of his party held the schoolmaster, (who had measured weapons before,) and the doctor and his friends restrained the secretary—both sides talking fast and furiously.

" Show thy warrant, officer ! show thy warrant."

" Does he think to bully us ?"

" Remember, we are Christians !"

" Gentlemen ! the supper ! the supper is laid hot—come to the supper—forbear fighting !" were exclamations that sounded out of the uproar, while the sheriff mounted the table and shouted rather than read the warrant. Then order was restored sufficiently to make out that only eight of the twenty were under arrest for misdemeanors that savored of treason. Among them were father Comstock and Gaffer Scates, but the schoolmaster was not included.

" Go, man," said Mistress Comstock, who had stood pale but tearless at the window's side ; " go, man, and die in jail ere thou abatest one jot or tittle of what thou hast said !"

" Bravo !" cried the prisoners.

" Silence : thou white-headed granny," cried the secretary.

" *Thou* couldst not buy my silence," retorted the dame, with spirit. " I am but a weak woman, but rather than surrender my free speech to thee, I'd go to the gibbet !"

CHAPTER X.

THE TYRANT'S SABBATH.

RUTH, finding her position unendurable at the Red Lion, (for Mistress Bean and others professed a holy horror at Captain Cameron's temerity in making himself the town's talk by rescuing Ruth from the ignominy of confession in the old church,) had accepted the invitation of rector Aldrich, who, it will be remembered, was the father of Margaret Aldrich, to make his house her home, and to take charge of little Imogene, their youngest born. Very thankfully she entered upon her duties, for she longed to be loved, if even only by a little child like Imogene. Besides, they trusted her, and it was so sweet to be trusted. She went to her new home on a Saturday. The next day was the Sabbath on which the Governor had determined to have service in the old meeting-house.

It was a strange sight for the Puritan Sabbath ! Impatient groups stood on the corner of the street leading to the church of the Mathers. Mounted men, who had come from a distance, not having heard the tyrannical edict of Sir Edmund Andros, reined in their impatient steeds while they heard the explanations and regrets of indignant townsmen, who gesticulated with more violence than grace, and shook their heads in a way that betokened deeply-outraged feeling. Men and women regarded the closed doors, some with tearful eyes and flushed faces, as they thought of the sacrilege (to them) permitted in the house of God. Ever and anon sounded on the air sonorous responses and solemn chanting. Close to the church stood soldiers on guard, ranged along each side, bearing themselves with a proudly regal air. In the center of the yard, the Governor's equipage, a high barouche, to which were harnessed two superb English stallions, a man in splendid livery on the box, glistened in its gold and varnish, and burnished coat-of-arms. More and more restless grew the excitable groups, and steadily the street filled up. The threatening voices sounded louder, and the low hum kept swelling to a deep, ominous thunder, subsiding only to break out into a fiercer depth.

Still, straight and stern stood the Governor's guard, looking neither to the right nor the left, scanning the faces directly before them with that same immobility of glance with which they would have regarded an advancing army.

"Saw you the strange lights in the heavens, last night, Master Rose?" asked an old man, who, with folded arms, had seemed more quiet than the rest.

"Ay! did I—the broadsword descending directly on this doomed town, and the blood-red flame that covered the sky like a mantle dipped in gore. It was a frightful spectacle, Goodman Browne, and did make my flesh creep."

"They say there was a horseman seen in the west, with a cross underneath him," added a young man, eagerly. "The Papistical worshipers may well tremble."

"The vengeance of the Lord!" muttered a stately-looking personage, with a long cue and a flowing beard. "Oh! would that this right arm was that of a Moses! Then would I smite the father of tyrannies."

"And my poor man lying in jail," muttered Mistress Comstock, pulling nervously at the strings of her great calash. "Well, it would mightily grieve him to see this sacrilege, I'm thinking."

"Turned out of the very house of God!" cried Mistress Scates, with angry gestures. "I would Scates were here!—bless me! how he would storm! I would that I might see this Governor caged like a wild beast!"

"Hear their Popish chanting!" they muttered, growing more and more restless as the minutes went on, and swaying toward the meeting-house.

"'Tis an hour past the time," said the schoolmaster, lifting his cocked hat and baring his broad brow to the wind.

"Let us enter and compel them to vacate," cried a hot-blooded youth, who had for some moments been striving to overthrow the equanimity of the British guard by prancing up and down so near them that the horse's hoofs almost touched the line made by their feet.

"Yes, we can bear this outrage no longer," came up from all parts of the vast crowd. "Are we dogs, to be trampled upon?"

"To the meeting-house! to the meeting-house!" was the subdued but fearful cry.

The soldiers stood, still straight and stern as ever, but a slight rattling sound was distinguishable running from end to end of their ranks. The crowd pressed together more eagerly yet—men, women, and even the children, seemed animated by the desire to defend their inalienable rights.

"Woe to them! woe!" cried the old man with white, waving locks, whose long beard and thoughtful face gave him a prophet-like dignity. "'Woe unto them that oppress my people, saith the Lord God.'"

An attack now seemed imminent. Defiance and religious zeal gloomed fiercely in the faces of the people. The rattling ran along the line of soldiers with a louder ring, and, for the first time, there was a slight movement perceptible in the persons of the guards. They seemed preparing for action, and grim smiles flitted across their faces.

When it seemed, at last, as if the whole force would swarm together (while the lolling coachman, the insolent footman, and one of the Governor's servants, vexed them with silent but expressive taunts,) and smite down the closed doors of their own beloved temple, a loud, deep voice was heard, saying:

"'Be strong and courageous; be not afraid nor dismayed, for the king of Assyria, nor for all the multitude that is with him. For there be more with us than with him.'

"'With him is an arm of flesh, but with us is the Lord our God to help us and to fight our battles.'"

Almost instantaneously a hush fell upon the people as they heard the beloved tones of their pastor, and Cotton Mather appeared in their midst, his face shining as if fresh from the baptism of prayer. They made no more threatenings while he was with them, and presently the church doors were thrown open, and the Governor-General, bowing haughtily, right and left, appeared with his secretary and the dignitaries of State. These were allowed to pass quietly—the guard drew into marching order—the secretary rode by his Excellency's barouche—the soldiers glittered into rank and file, and the people entered their meeting-house, expecting, almost, to see the *mene, mene,* of the former sacrilegious gathering upon its walls.

A gloom had settled over that body of religious worshippers. Their rights had been wrested from them, their protests treated with contempt; while the absence of certain resonant sounds from the choir-gallery reminded them that in the pestilent jail were incarcerated some of their most worthy brethren, and an unuttered but not an unregistered vow went up to heaven.

Another thing had grieved them. They had seen Ruth Margerie among the Episcopals—the pale Ruth, who, at the cold, averted looks cast at her from all who had gathered there, held down her burning face, clinging only the more devotedly to the dainty, ungloved hand of Imogene, who, in a sweetly serious way, smiled on the threatening faces about her, even as she drew closer to Ruth, as if to protect and to be protected. Not one of all that company, professing Christ, save perhaps Mistress Comstock, had either charity or compassion for Ruth. In their suspicious eyes, she was marked as plainly as if she carried the " mark of the beast" upon her brow. " It shows that she has sinned," they said ; " she, going from the church of her fathers to the ceremonials of a Papistical service !"

So Ruth was, quietly and without compunction, made over to the devil.

3

CHAPTER XI.

RUTH IN HER NEW HOME, BUT CALLED TO ANOTHER TRIAL.

" COME, dance with me, Ruthy."

" I don't know how to dance, darling."

" Oh ! it's easy—just go so—and so—and turn so and so;" and the fairy-like body tripped and whirled—flitting now to shadow, then into the sunshine, and back again into Ruth's arms almost before she knew it—then off again with breezy, noiseless motion, till the young girl gazed breathless, fearful that the beautiful thing would vanish.

" *Now* you'll come and dance with me—I've teached you," and a glad laugh broke forth.   " Sing again—come."

" My darling, I would only be clumsy, and throw you down ; besides, I love to look at you."

" Then sing to me—sing that pretty little tune;" and the child dropped on her knees, folded her white arms over Ruth's lap, and raised her haunting eyes, so bright and beau‑ tiful, that Ruth almost lost herself looking at them.

" Yes, I'll sing for you," murmured Ruth ; " now listen:

> " I have found a little jewel,
>   Heaven-white and heaven-blue;
> I will wear it in my bosom,
>   As the stately maidens do.

> " No, not as the stately maidens,
>   With their pride of glass and gold,
> For their richest, rarest baubles
>   Are not half so rich and old.

> " As my iris-colored jewel;
>   From God's hand its beauty grew,
> His own lightest breathing made it
>   Heaven-white and heaven-blue.

> " So I'll wear this precious jewel,

[Here little Imogene chimed in, her pretty hands keeping time as they were folded over Ruth's lap.]

> Wear it ever till I'm old;
> 'Tis a drop of heaven's glory,
>   Set in heaven's unfading gold."

"I know what it is—I know what it is; it's *truth!* you told me so," cried the child, clapping her little palms. Then she laid her head down softly and was very silent. Hearing Ruth sigh, she looked up hastily.

"Have you got the heart-ache again?" she asked.

Ruth, sighing, had told her half-playfully one day, that she had the heart-ache, and at every cloud that saddened her face, the question was repeated.

"Oh no, darling; but why did you sob so this morning, and why did you tell such a terrible story?"

She held her caressingly with one hand, and touched the golden curls flittingly with the points of her fingers, as if they were sacred and to be handled with reverence.

"Because"—that distant, awe-filled, visionary look came over the childish face. "Because I saw the wicked man, and he tried to take you away from me."

"How did he look, darling?"

"He had great long curls," said the child, stretching out one of her own bright ringlets; "and he looked like the dark lady. Oh! I guess he was the dark lady's father, for (she stooped forward, her eyes dilating,) there was something wicked over his shoulder!"

Ruth felt a shiver at these words. She did not doubt the child had seen what she said.

"You won't go away with the dark man and leave Imogene—go away on the dark water—will you, Ruthy?" she cried, with most impassioned earnestness; then, with her usual flitting, springing motion, she was now on this side of Ruth, now on that, patting Ruth's forehead, patting her cheeks, kissing her, smiling, humming, dancing.

The room was square, of large dimensions, low-ceiled and tastefully furnished. A warm-looking carpet, with bright-red tints showing everywhere—cut into strips by mother—woven by an old Scotch weaver in Pudding lane—quite covered the floor. It glowed now under the light of the crimson sunshine as well as the cheerful hickory fire. In a recess, at one end, stood a low bed and a child's crib. The latter was no longer in use, for Imogene had outgrown it. Since Ruth had come, she had slept in her arms—her little head pillowed on her breast, over her heart.

Rector Aldrich and his wife were, in character, of the true
spiritual type—following their Master blamelessly—*practicing*
as well as preaching his precepts—loving every manifestation of his perfect love. So, on all sides, Ruth was surrounded
by the most gentle beings. It was a household of love, and
Ruth would have been happy but for the apparent stain upon
her hitherto unspotted reputation.

Even Cotton Mather felt that Ruth was no longer to be
considered one of the ".household of faith." Why had she
gone over to the Episcopals ? Why did she not apply to him
and to his family in her trouble ? He did not dream that
Ruth was afraid of him—that his awfully severe denunciations
had made him seem to her something too sacred for common
mortals to approach. He did not dream how she trembled—
loving him in her fearful way though she did—when he
approached her. Yet he was not, in his home, a stern or a
harsh man. He had a gentle soul and a tender spirit ; but,
from a mistaken sense of the greatness of his mission, he
clothed himself in a dignity and severity that were appalling
to the timid, and made even the men of vigorous intellect bend
with a conscious humility, and a something very like dread, in
his presence.

Those glorious old-time preachers of the Word! Perish
the pen that would do them dishonor ; but had they studied
Christ more, and creeds and the Fathers less, surely their
hearts had been filled with the love of God, and their gentle-
ness might have constrained maids like Ruth to sit with reverence, not with terror, in their presence.

But Minister Aldrich, in spite of many troubles, was a
cheerful man, and his wife scarcely spoke without a sunny
smile. She, in the long evenings, sung to the music of the
spinnet, and sometimes Ruth sung. They said she had a
wondrous voice.

Since the imprisonment of Sir John Willie, Margaret and
Eleanor came oftener to the parsonage. The young secretary
of Cotton Mather, or, as he was called in those days, "the
clark," frequently made one of their number. Of late, the
sunbeam-face of Eleanor Saltonstall, with its rippling smiles
and curls—its changeful, gleeful light—its blooming cheeks,
seemed to have a new attraction for him. Seeing this, perhaps

rather, *feeling* it, Eleanor grew more radiant, more charming.

Margaret always sought Ruth out, and the two would talk together of indifferent things, till, edging around all the streets of Boston, they made a full stop at last in Prison lane, before the stone jail—when both would enter—and henceforth it was not Ruth the portionless orphan, with the Governor's stately niece, but Ruth the suffering, the loving; Ruth the sister made so by the sacredness of affection.

On that beautiful spring morning, Ruth heard the trumpet and the tramp of the warrior-horse that always carried the Governor's messengers when there was any thing of importance on hand. Little Imogene was wild at the sight of the soldier and his bright uniform. Ruth stood with the eager-eyed child, whose curls the light breeze blew all over her milk-white forehead, at an open window. The crowd was gathering, hurrying by on the sidewalk—children, men and women; the townsmen sometimes lifting their hats at the shout:

"God save the king!"

Suddenly a hand was upstretched from the crowd, and a rough brown paper fell within the window, at Ruth's feet.

The sensitive child turned quickly toward Ruth, who had picked up and now held the paper in her hand. Imogene had seen neither the movement nor the missive, but all the glad light faded from her face. She said, sadly, as her lips quivered and her eyes filled with tears:

"Take me down."

Then she clasped Ruth's gown tightly, and followed her everywhere, with troubled glances—nor could Ruth find a minute to read the paper until she left the room.

At sight of the writing her heart beat almost to bursting, and, through hot, anguished tears she traced the rude writing. Thus it read:

"*Ruth, come again; only once more, between nine and ten. Come to the little cove next to the wharf where the ferry-boat lies. Ruth, for God's sake, don't fail me. They don't ferry over after six, so there's no danger of you being seen if you are careful. Ruth, I shall never see you again—this is my last prayer—oh! Ruth, don't fail me.*"

"**Another bitter, bitter trial!**" issued from Ruth's **pale lips,**

as she sat, white and nerveless—sat without moving till the
sweet, silvery voice of Imogene was heard calling her.

"I'm coming, dear."

She could not meet the calm, questioning eyes of the little
child, so she smiled without looking at her, and finding an
opportunity, slipped the paper in the flame. But her sad face
betrayed her every movement. She tried once or twice to
break the unnatural hush of the room, for Imogene never
spoke, but hovered near with many a little noiseless caress,
and seemed not to care to play at all.

. A note came near night, informing Ruth that the minister
and his wife would not be home till ten o'clock, perhaps later,
and charging Ruth to look after Imogene. They had been
gone all day on some important business connected with a will
that had lately been submitted to a contest in England.

"Worse and worse," murmured Ruth, almost wringing her
hands. "I must not leave *her*—I must see *him*. But she will
be here—safe, sleeping; and I shall never see him again. Oh!
yes, I must, I *must* go—he will keep me but a moment, when
I tell him what I have left. I must go and trust her to God!"

CHAPTER XII.

THE EXPERIENCES OF A NIGHT.

By every little artifice that Ruth could think of, she tried to
lure Imogene to her bed. The child had never before shown
so strange a contrariety. She refused to have her clothes removed, though in her own sweet, coaxing way, and still sat
by the fire, her great, unearthly eyes fastened upon Ruth.

"I don't want to sleep—you'll go with the naughty man,"
she said, as, again and again, Ruth importuned. At last Imogene compromised. "You may put my bed-gown over my
frock," she said, "if it will make you feel better—but I musn't
go to sleep; I *must* keep wide awake!"

And certainly her spirit-like eyes justified her assertion, for
they looked indeed as if they were compelled to keep awake.

But, long after her usual hour, the little creature began to grow weary. Her dear head fell over on Ruth's knee, and there they sat, Ruth scarce daring to breathe, while a sweet slumber gained upon the weary, watchful Imogene.

"God has sent you for my good angel, sweet darling.' murmured Ruth, taking her up tenderly and laying her on the bed. Imprinting a kiss upon the dewy lips, she knelt down, asked God to forgive her if in what she was doing there was aught of wrong. Then, tying on her bonnet and folding a large shawl about her, she left, without speaking to the servants, by a back entrance, saying to herself, as she drew the door to, carefully, "I will certainly be back so soon, nobody shall miss me."

There was a moon and a cloudless sky, so that the streets looked very light. But few people were abroad, but, in hastily turning a corner, Ruth came in contact with a gentleman, so that he caught her to save her from a fall.

"Ruth!" he said, sternly—for it was Cotton Mather, on his way from the Red Lion. "Unhappy girl! why do I find thee here at this late hour?"

"I—am—going—" murmured Ruth, faintly, overcome with her confusion.

"Alas! I fear, going that road from which no prayers can bring thee back. Miserable child! can nothing save thee? Art thou lost! lost! forever lost?"

There was fever in Ruth's veins, fierce fever on her cheek. Could she have dropped there and sunk into the earth before him! Oh! to be thought of as she knew by his words, his manner, what he must think! and she powerless to defend herself. It was agony! She tried to pass him.

"My poor maid!" he said, and it seemed as if there were tears in his very voice. "I mourn thee as a shepherd would mourn a lost lamb—but I fear Satan hath possession of thee. Go, unfortunate—but when, in the misery to which, sooner or later, sin must bring thee—when even those who smile on thee leave thee to the torture of the undying worm—then send for thy minister whose counsel thou hast set at naught, and he will gladly come and kneel by thee and commend thee to Heaven's mercy."

It seemed to Ruth as if she was turning to marble as he

spoke thus. Her tongue felt palsied, or she would have cried
out what her heart wailed, "Oh! my God, has no one mercy
on me?"

For a moment she stood where he had left her—her head
like one burning coal, her feet chilled as the stones they
pressed—her hands ice. But this was no time for tears, for
regrets—we will not say for a guiltless shame—*that* had per-
meated every fiber of her frame.

"He thinks me lost! he despises me! Oh! to bear *this*
also!"

A few hot tears fell to the ground—a few sighs ascended to
the pitying Deity, and she hurried forward, meeting now and
then some suspicious loiterer, who stopped to look, but soon
went on his way. Nearly breathless, and no little frightened,
she gained the place she sought, a sheltered point of land,
running out far into the water, and made secluded by the
thick trunks of a few trees on one side, and a pile of rough
lumber on the other. Here she sunk down, literally speaking,
nearly dead; for her fright, the meeting with Cotton Mather,
and the secrecy, were too much for her, and, with her hand
held against a heavily-beating heart, she listened for coming
footsteps. She had not to listen long. A man emerged from
the shadow, very cautiously, and in the moonlight appeared,
to her excited imagination, of gigantic height and dimensions.

"Is this Ruth?" he asked, his voice issuing thickly from
under the cloak in which he was muffled.

"You wished to see me; speak quickly, for pity's sake.
Here is a little money—not so much as the last time—but all
I have. Take it if it will aid you, only let me go; don't
keep me. Good heavens! you are not he!" and Ruth, springing to her feet, stood ready to fly.

"He is very sick—dangerously so," said the man, softening
his tone; "desperately hurt, and the poor fellow calls you
from morning till night."

"Where is he?" Ruth asked, trembling from head to
foot.

"On one of the islands, not far out in the harbor. My
boat will be here presently."

"You can not think"—Ruth's voice was nearly lost in her
terror; "you can not think I would go with—a—stranger."

A wild, undefinable dread filled her heart—she stepped back a pace or two.

"If you would see him in this world, you must go with me; it will not take long—only an hour; I will bring you back immediately. Poor soul! to hear him cry for you! to hear his voice, so piteous! to see him hold out his hand for a grasp of yours—I say it's a sorrowful sight. I shouldn't wonder if there's something on his mind he wants to tell you before he dies."

"Before he dies!" echoed Ruth, in a low, awe-struck tone. "Oh! is it so bad as that? What shall I do? How did it happen?" she asked tearfully, a moment after.

"It happened last night—no matter how," was the answer.

"Was—was he—fighting?"

The words struggled out of her mouth—a thrilling horror vailed them.

"He got a devilish bad cut!" muttered the man to himself.

"And—*who* are you?" asked Ruth, her terror increasing and nearly mastering her.

"I—why—I'm nobody you need to be frightened at. If you'll keep it a secret, I'll let you into an item or two regarding myself—I'll whisper to you that I'm the Governor's nephew. What do you think of that? I'm the brother of handsome Margaret Aldrich. What do you think of that, too?"

At that moment Ruth caught sight of his face and grew faint. A bold, defiant face it was, but its beauty was reckless and sensual; and, as his cloak flew open, he stooping toward her, she saw a long beard and curls of a jetty black hanging over his collar.

Imogene's vision—Imogene's terror, flashed over her soul. She did not breathe for a space, so appalled was she by the remembrance of the child's words—the child's watching care. The man stood impatient, ready to spring toward her—watching her with a tiger-like glance—ready also to spring toward the boat, over whose tardiness he muttered many an imprecation.

"Maybe you doubt me?" he said, taking a position to intercept her if she should attempt to escape. "Maybe you don't want to go with me?"

Ruth's faculties were wide awake now.

"Oh! yes, I do ;" she lifted her pale face—in her soul she prayed to be delivered from this great danger. "Yes—you say he calls for me—my place is at his side. Oh! if but this moment I were there!"

"You'd hardly know him," returned Captain Bill, now quite reassured; "cut all to pieces—the fellows fought like demons," he muttered to himself, in low, excited tones.

Suddenly, with an awful distinctness, like a cold, sharp blow from some unseen hand, it flashed over her that here was one of the murderers of the poor soldiers on board of Captain Cameron's ship. She remembered how the awful news was told—that the men must have made almost superhuman efforts to save themselves—that the deck was slippery with blood. It chilled her heart to the very core—she grew too faint to support herself, and sunk down upon a chance-seat, a drifted log, covered with dry sea-weed. Had he who sent for her borne a hand in that night's hellish work? Then would she steel her heart against him forever.

She looked up; Captain Bill was watching her keenly. Regaining her presence of mind, she folded her hands together, exclaiming, with no simulated anguish:

"Will the boat *never* come? Oh! how long."

The man was thoroughly deceived by her words, her manner.

"Wait," he said; "I have not dared use it, but I have a whistle here. I'll just go to the corner; you sit where you are, and in less than five minutes, I'll warrant, we have the boat, (and I'll have you,") he added, in an undertone.

In less than five minutes Ruth fell like a stone within Mistress Bean's kitchen!

CHAPTER XIII.

IMOGENE LOST AND RESTORED.

THE poor widow, what with her fright previously and the altogether unexpected entrance of one whose absence she had been lamenting all day, knew hardly which way to turn—whether to fly from or to take charge of the terrified, half-lifeless creature at her feet.

Mistress Comstock, however, acted with greater energy; and, while the widow stood wondering and lamenting, she had forced a few drops of brandy between her pale lips, and Ruth could support herself.

"Who will go home with me—who?" she cried, wildly. "I must fly this moment, for I left her alone."

"Don't think of going out to-night, Ruth," said Mistress Bean; "you must stay here. You look like a ghost, child—where have you been? what frightened you? Ruth Margerie, whatever are we to think of you? What a strange being you are!"

"I know you feel so—I know others feel so," replied Ruth, forcing herself to be calm. "I have borne enough already to wish myself in the grave beside my mother," she sobbed, woefully; but, in a moment, dashing the tears from her eyes, she cried again, "Is there no one to go home with me? They left little Imogene in my charge, and her parents will come back; and if *they* find me missing, (she wrung her hands,) then I shall have no friends—no more—forever!"

"There's the schoolmaster," suggested Mistress Comstock; "I'll go ask him;" and away went the motherly old soul. When she came back to help Ruth to place her bonnet more evenly, to pin her shawl more closely, she pressed her trembling hands.

"Always remember that *I* don't think ill of thee, cosset," she said, passing her arm around the little frame that trembled so.

"Oh! thank you! thank you!" sobbed Ruth. She was so grateful for a kind word.

The old schoolmaster was quite willing to accompany Ruth, and she, as she leaned on his arm, thought how beautiful it would be! how it would brighten her path with sunshine, if she had only a father like him!

Alas! with that thought came the keenest pain of her life!

Thoroughly wretched, Ruth hastened to her room, and had but just placed her things away when the minister and his wife came in. Ruth stood smoothing her hair at the mirror, wondering what they would think of her pinched, white face, when Mrs. Aldrich entered, with a light step.

"Oh, Ruth!" she said, in her sweet, cheerful way, "I was going to tell you "—then came a pause, followed by a quick, piercing cry:

"Where's my child?"

Ruth flew to the bedside. The clothes were thrown back, the pillows disarranged—there was nobody there!

"My God! where's my child?" cried Mrs. Aldrich, frightened at Ruth's fearful face, and so loudly that Mr. Aldrich came hurrying in.

Ruth neither spoke nor moved.

"My child! my child! Parris," cried the mother, in the same hollow, muffled voice, "go look! go in the servants' rooms—in our room—everywhere. Ruth Margerie, look! why don't *you* look? Did you leave the room? Speak, girl! or have *you* stolen my precious babe?"

But to all these passionate cries Ruth could make no answer; she could not speak. A dull, roaring sound—a distant, deadened rumbling, as if she heard the tumult of far-off waves, was all she was conscious of. Mrs. Aldrich seemed frightened for her, and pushing her a little, made her go backward, until she came to a chair, where she sat down. Forever and forever that ringing in her ears—that cold, passionless, stony feeling! Was this eternity?

One hour went by—two hours. She had not moved, not so much as an eyelash, when, with a flash of light as if the heavens had opened, there stood Imogene—then she was on her lap, fondling, murmuring, kissing.

This was so strange! It was something to make one laugh, and she did laugh—oh! how long! wildly! madly! Laughed till everybody cried, and little Imogene ran to her mother, grieving.

That awakened her to consciousness. The bewilderment faded slowly, and she saw, standing very near her, a man, roughly-garbed, who was looking from her to Imogene, apparently wondering what it all meant.

"You see, sir," he began, telling his story, "merchant Stokes hired me to watch outside o' his shop—this here murder here making folks suspicious. So, as I stood there—it might be nigh ten or so—I sees something that made my flesh creep come round the corner. I thought it was a spirit, with its white dress and long, dancing hair, and I holds my breath with mortal fear as it come on. Presently I felt a little cold hand tetch me, and even then I wern't sartin whether it were flesh and blood, till a little voice says:

" 'Please carry me home.'

" 'Then you *are* a mortal being,' says I ; for the face was so unearthly, 'specially with the moon shining on it, that I thought maybe 'twas an angel. Says she :

" 'I'm Imogene, and I've been looking for Ruth. Won't you take me home ?'

"Says I, ' Where's your home, little one, and who is Ruth ?' and I begun to remember then who it was.

" 'I'm little Imogene Aldrich,' was the reply—and I never see nothin' of that bigness look so womanly. 'Ruth takes care of me,' said she, 'and I waked up, and Ruth wasn't there ; so I came to find her, but Ruth's gone home now.'

"I declare t' ye, I begun to feel my flesh creep ag'in, and my hair rise, for I'd heered that the child was uncommon ; so I jest took her up and she put her arms round my neck, and lay like a little dove, cuddling down to my bosom, while I brought her. Well, sir, p'raps I may look a little soft-hearted crying here, but I had a child, sir—gone to heaven now—that used to cuddle jest so. But *she's* mysterus !" he added, solemnly. "I hope you'll keep her."

When Ruth came to entire consciousness of the past—of the present—the man was gone. Mrs. Aldrich was weeping tears of joy over the child, who had fallen into a sweet slumber.

"I wonder how far she had been in the dark night?" she

murmured, laying the little one in her bed, with many a silent
kiss. "And what went you, for, Ruth?—we trusted you so
entirely," she added, in a regretful voice.

"Ruth can clear herself, I know," spoke the minister, with
confidence.

And Ruth did clear herself. In a low, tearful tone, trembling like a leaf as she talked, interrupted often with gushing
tears and sighs of heart-anguish, Ruth *did* clear herself tri-
umphantly.

CHAPTER XIV.

A TYRANT'S COURT OF JUSTICE.

THE trial of the prisoners came off in less than a week.
To their astonishment they found that another had been
added to their number—Captain Cameron, the lover of Ruth
Margerie. He being a free-spoken man, and disliked by the
Governor and his tools, it was an easy thing to trump up a
charge against him. The jewel-merchant—with whom, it
will be remembered, he had quarreled on his passage from
England—had been most assiduously at work to have him
arrested. As *witchcraft* was the usual resource, when other
charges failed, so now he was accused of possessing that
power, and of using it to the disadvantage of those whom he
disliked. Then, too, the murder in the harbor had taken
place on board his ship, and, it was hoped, might be traced to
him, by those who hated him.

Father Comstock, Gaffer Scates, and their aiders and abettors, were dispatched with little ceremony, for several months'
imprisonment, and with small show of law, or even of dignity.

Among the spectators who sat near the bench, were the
Governor's secretary and one other obnoxious individual, who,
it was evident, intended to enjoy the discomfiture of the accused, for they well knew what law would be dealt out to
them. Returning the frowning looks of the people with contemptuous smiles and haughty gestures, the secretary would

sometimes speak with his companion in words so loud and so insulting that they roused an honest indignation in every manly breast.

During the examination for witchcraft, the young ship master's eye would occasionally flash, and his free, indignant spirit break out into words of defiance, for which he was severely reproved. During the course of the examination, several old women of haggish appearance were summoned to testify that the young master had bewitched them. Had they been younger by some scores of years, there might have been a show of truth in their assertions. One of the crones averred that her son had lately died of a strange disease, having been a foremast hand on his ship, and that he declared with his dying breath that Master Cameron had bewitched him.

This, to the sage wisdom assembled in the body of the justices, was triumphant evidence, especially as two of the old beldames confessed that they had once had dealings with the devil and knew all the signs.

"Abominable liars!" cried the Captain, at last losing all patience, as they proceeded to relate some matters for whose details they were indebted solely to imagination.

"I'll back him up there!" murmured Marmaduke Catch-cod.

"Silence!" cried the justices, angrily.

"Darest thou, rash young man, to call that superstition which Holy Scripture declareth to be of the devil?" demanded Justice Bullivant, his little black eyes twinkling wrath in mimic flashes into the face that awed him, so severe was its beauty. "Then thou art an infidel, and deservest no mercy. In our minds thy case is clear, thou God-forsaken man! We have already sufficient evidence to commit thee to the flames or the rope, but will, in consideration of thy youth, remand thee to prison, there to await another trial."

Up spoke a wizen-faced old man, who passed for a lawyer: "Perhaps, your Honor, the maid called Ruth Margerie could tell thee more of yonder devil's dealings. I have heard that she doth confess to being bewitched by him."

"It is a lie! a naked and infamous lie!" cried the Captain, turning white.

" We fine thee one hundred pounds for contempt of court, and order that the maid Margerie be summoned before us as soon as she may be found," said Judge Bullivant.

Captain Cameron straightened himself—bit his lip—while quivering chin, maddened brow, burning cheeks, purple where they were white before, gleaming eyes full of vengeful flame, told how fearfully he was shaken at this outrage. But he was powerless *as yet*—with all his strength, courage and auger, he was powerless. Meantime it was suggested that the sailor be called upon the stand. Catchcod felt in his generous breast a glow of sympathy—a strong indignation, that made him, for the time, fearless and reckless of his own safety.

" Come hither, man ; who art thou ?   What's thy name ?"

" Name, may it please your big-wigs," said the man, conscious that he must address them by some title commensurate with their dignity, " it's Catchcod—commonly called Catchcod, Duke of Marma."

" Lower thy tone, man," said the Chief Justice, frowning as he spoke.   " What is your trade ?"

" Trade ! Lord love you, I ain't got no trade in particular ; but I can curl you, cut you, shave you, trim you, pill you, book you and cook you."

" Be careful how you answer for sport, fellow," said one of the justices, seeing the people, so quiet and threatening before, begin to laugh.   " Confine yourself to the questions asked.   I wish to know, in plain terms, if you're a sailor, and, if so, in *what* have you sailed ?"

" Am I a sailor ?   Yes, your big-wigs, I *are*, (with emphasis,) and as to what I has sailed in, (here he took a deep breath,) I has sailed in a k'now—a ketch—a 'oy—a buss—a scow—a b'ark (that's a bloody man-o-war, mind ye,") he added, talking as fast as he could rattle, his one eye on the ceiling— " a gig—a runny—a dingy—a bumboat—a cobble—a punt—a coy—a kedge—a outrigger catamaran—gracious ! you ought to see Catamaran Jack.   Whiz and splash, and he's flip-flop clean onto your decks—any thing but clean, though, come to think on't.   Then there's the furrin things in outlandish ports, sich as the fl'st—the kick (caique)—the galley fl'st—the dagger —the howker—the—"

" Silence !" thundered the justice, annoyed at the open

laughter all over the room. "Witness will stop. Witness will continue on the stand," he added, as Marmaduke, thinking the word an order to take his seat, was backing out with dextrous movements.

"I'm bang-up, your Honor," replied the sailor. "By the jumping Jupiter! this is worse nor being in the Indys a eating *ghee.*"

"Why dost not answer more tersely?" asked the Chief Justice, with authority.

"Tersely! that's a sentence I'm onacquainted with," muttered the prisoner; "but if I understand you right—I don't burn a candle at both ends; that ain't my way."

"Why don't you talk common sense?" asked a lawyer.

"Rats in the upper story, sir," he answered, tapping his forehead in such a ludicrous way that an explosive laugh sounded all over the room.

"We must do something to bring the prisoner to proper respect, your Honor, or this trial can not progress. I—"

"Tide it over, Judge—tide it over," cried Marmaduke, winking his one eye, thinking it fine sport to set the people laughing.

"The constable will put this man in the stocks, immediately," said Justice Bullivant, his face growing red. "There shall he remain twenty-four hours for contempt of court."

"Lud, sir!" cried Marmaduke, startled into sobriety; "I thought I was talking as fine as a carrot. I'll double my marrow-bones t'ye, sir, if that'll do any good. I don't want to be stockined, sir—what'll it boot?"

But Catchcod was promptly taken off and hurried to the stocks.

The justices did not altogether like the appearance of things. The expression of every countenance in the room was a riddle they could not solve—it seemed like that of one man, and he determined, defiant, but forbearing. Captain Cameron writhed in his seat as Ruth was ushered into the crowded court-room. The secretary had been playing with the hilt of his sword, occasionally, however, pausing to address his friends with a smile and a shrug. His insolence was palpable, and though Captain Cameron had scarcely thought of him before, he shuddered now as he gazed that way. Oh!

to bring that rare beauty before the corrupt gaze of the boast-
ful, licentious secretary! Oh! to have her modest, lady-like
bearing made the subject of his free scrutiny! It fired his
blood and maddened his brain. He grew sick and dizzy as
he saw how quickly the bold eye lighted with admiration—
marked her every movement—heard him whisper his coarse
approval of her looks.

It was very evident that the Governor's secretary was aston-
ished, not only at Ruth's loveliness, but the perfect ease and
dignity with which, after the first few moments, Ruth accom-
modated herself to the circumstances in which she had
innocently been placed. The blush still dyed her cheek—her
eyes were downcast and vailed by their long lashes, (they had
fallen at first sight of the Captain,) but she did not falter in a
single reply, until one of the insolent lawyers propounded
such questions that embarrassed her by their coarseness. Then
she clasped her hands together, and, with a sweet, piteous look,
appealed to every man before her, saw no mercy in their case-
hardened faces, and hid her burning blushes while her frame
shook to falling.

"In the name of God and humanity!" cried Captain Cameron, springing to his feet.

"The young woman is ill," said a voice in the crowd—and
cries of "Shame! insult!" and words of deeper, darker por-
tent, fell from the lips of the crowd. The storm was ready
to burst. Secure as they imagined themselves, the justices
dared not go on, for, of late, there had been so many threats
and rumors that they could not but see which way the tide of
popular feeling was turning. Therefore they released the half-
fainting girl.

But what was the horror of Captain Cameron to see the
secretary, after a few whispered words, rise and leave the
room the moment Ruth was led out. The sight nerved him
to desperation. He was ready for an outbreak, and he saw
encouragement in the knit brows and firm lips that surrounded
him. He determined, at that moment, to achieve his liberty.
He was remanded back to jail—but the hearing of the next
and last case was scarcely begun when the officer in whose
charge the Captain had been placed rushed into court, bruised
and bloody, and yelling:

" The prisoner! the prisoner, please your Honors, has escaped, and left me with these marks."

There was instant commotion all over the room.

" He knocked me down and ran, and not so much as one lifted a hand, though many of the townsmen saw it," cried the constable. " As soon as I was up, your Honors, I tried to run, but my bruises forbid."

" That's the way to do it," said a sharp voice. " Three cheers for Cameron."

On that, every man sprung to his feet, and the crowd, giving one wild shout, in defiance of the rules and to the consternation of the assembled dignitaries, began their comments, talking fast and furiously, while the justices, shocked at this new sign of insubordination, vociferated in vain for order. The court broke up in the most reckless confusion.

CHAPTER XV.

CATCHCOD IN THE STOCKS.

WHEN it was known that the stocks, of late unseen, were to be put in requisition again, a rabble crowd collected speedily. Children and half-grown lads followed the jolly sailor, who, now that he was fully committed, gave his lively tongue and his livelier fancy as much scope as he pleased.

" Here goes Catchcod, Duke of Marma, to be stockinged," he cried, half turning to the grimacing, shouting procession. " Look here, Mister," he added, as the people pressed closely, " don't you call this taking to one's heels? Sho! I'm clean gastered; I'm running away from the devil, and his imps are after me."

He was fastened to the instrument with considerable satisfaction by the constable, who, as he came round, grinned at the figure he cut, his head and hands thrust through corresponding holes, his one eye leering shockingly, his hair sticking like splinters to the wood.

" Well," said Catchcod, " you like it, don't you? I'm

patience kicking on a moniment. It's all very well, only I'd
like something softer to kick, say you, Mr. constable."

At this all the little boys roared and took off their caps with
unbounded respect for the plucky prisoner.

"This is a nice place to take an observation," cried Catchcod; "a werry nice place to see stars," he added, trying to
lift his head. "Come, you varlets, (as his humorous fancy
took a rebound,) here's a pig in a poke—going cheap—who'll
buy ?"

"Fits like a glove, don't it ?" he asked innocently, of a
portly personage, who stopped to examine the instrument.
"Say, d'ye know why I'm like a man beginning in business?
'Cause I'm just sot up, and got a good deal on my hands
likewise."

In a few moments the Governor and his suite passed by.
Having heard about the tumult, they were on the way to the
court-house. His Excellency paused a single moment, curious
to see who was undergoing punishment. His face lighted up
as he recognized the man.

"Hulloa! Rusty-cuss!" cried Catchcod, depending on his
treacherous memory—spasmodically shutting his fingers as if
pulling his forelock, and ducking his head to the best of his
ability, while his one eye rolled unceasingly—"I hope your
exodus is partic'larly well. I'm agreeable except I ain't used
to a fancy dress in public, and it's 'noying to a modest man.
I say, influenza, won't your ecclesiasticus libertize a poor sailor
cuss, as he did duty on the ocean over ten years? I always
helps a lame dog over the fence, Guv'ner."

"Silence! you fool," exclaimed one of the Governor's suite,
as his Excellency strode haughtily away.

"You shet up!" was the independent rejoinder.

The children, little and large, stood by, grinning in delighted
admiration, that was heightened to intense enthusiasm when
the imprisoned man began to crow with stentorian lungs—
making each "cock-a-doodle-do" to rival its predecessor in
ear-splitting sound. Presently, one would have thought the
streets full of bantam roosters, for what Catchcod had begun
the little urchins kept up indefatigably, while Catchcod laughed
till the tears ran out of his one queer eye. Adapting his ver·
satile genius to successive imitations, he not only crowed, but

barked mewed and roared, till the vicinity of the stocks seemed converted into a vast menagerie, more noisy than musical.

Suddenly Catchcod paused, and, with a look of the deepest solemnity, said slowly, and with an elongated countenance :

"I don't never recollect 'aving my 'ands occupied that my nose didn't itch. It's always sure to be so. Will that 'ar little boy with the smock-frock, and knees on both patches, scratch my nose for me ?"

A yell followed the delivery of this sentimental speech, and the prisoner was assailed with a dozen hands, all ready to perform the agreeable office with more unction than was required, and which, now, he was powerless to prevent. They climbed upon the stocks—they shouted in his ears—they pulled his hair, until he begged for mercy.

"Avast there—that'll do—avast ! fall back, and I'll sing ye a song—fall back if ye want to hear me sing."

The crowd stood off for a moment, waiting with looks of expectation, while Catchcod, hemming innumerable times, and taking the pitch in as many keys, broke out in the following admirable impromptu :

> "I'm a going away
>   Far over the sea,
> And the country I sail for
>   It is Ameri*kee ;*
> But now I've anchored here,
>   I wish I was away,
> For a pesky mean place
>   Is Ameri*kay.*

> "If a man says a word,
>   Why, they'll put him in the stocks,
> A very queer thing,
>   That the constable locks—
> And the Guv'ner he looks
>   Like aristocrackit cur,
> And he won't let his subjec'
>   Call him Sur.

> "So I'll call him the great
>   Ecclesiastic*uss,*
> Who, for a little thing,
>   Makes a mighty big fuss ;
> And if there ain't in pickle
>   For him a big rod,
> Then you may call me everything
>   But Duke of Catchcod !

" If I didn't know he was in court, I'd be bound to say there's Master Cameron making off, down there. Hurrah! cry out, little boys, it's him—he's free! he's free! Hurrah! hurrah!"

The rabble, not understanding him, were making preparation to coerce him into singing another song, by initiating sundry moves toward his nose, which bore marks of rude handling, when the constable appeared, and, with a long, flexible ratan, dispersed the children, who took their several ways for home with great reluctance, throwing back, by way of a gentle remonstrance, bits of earth and splinters that were, some of them, so unfortunate as to come in contact with Catchcod's hardy face.

CHAPTER XVI.

RUTH ASKED FOR A KISS.

NEARER and nearer drew the time for the Governor's overthrow. The best citizens of Boston were imprisoned on the most trivial charges. Freedom of speech was denied, and taxes assessed till the spirit of the colonists revolted, and they swore that they would be rid of a Governor who was the tool of a tyrant, especially as England was under a better rule. Accordingly they held meetings in secret, and spread their dissatisfaction far and wide, until all were ready for determined action.

Ruth went often to see the good wife of Gaffer Comstock, whose term of imprisonment had not yet expired.

"Now, Heaven forgive me, child!" said Mistress Comstock, as Ruth stepped from the little entry into the keeping-room, "if I wish ill to the Governor. Didst say, Ruth, that they drove the justices from the town-house? Dear! dear! I hear no news since my good man is taken. Well—and the Captain has got his liberty too—wonderful! And thou wert coming by?"

Ruth repeated what she had seen, while Goody Comstock

busied herself in pouring some savory mess into a deep kettle, and then securing the lid, she handed it to Ruth.

"God bless thee, cosset," she said, "and tell me again that thou dost not fear. That pleasant minister Aldrich! Surely I can think no evil, even of an Episcopal, if he hath such a heart as thou sayest. How kind in him to get a permit for thee of that bad man, the Governor! Alack, one can not help having had relations sometimes! Ah! my poor Goodman Comstock! I warrant thee he has not relished one mouthful of his food in that terrible place. Tell him his old Mistress sent him a chicken-pie, and took master pains in the making of it—for she felt as if he was forsaken-like;" the dame faltered and put her check apron up to her eyes for a brief moment, then threw it down again and smiled through her tears.

"I don't think they'll harm him, cosset, otherwise than that damp place may bring on his rheumatics. Dost hear what a rumpus, child? Where can all the people be going to? See, there passes Governor Bradstreet—dear, saintly old gentleman! he hath seen near a hundred. Do look again, Ruth! The boys have red ribbons in their button-holes, and carry clubs. Thou dost not think there will be open fighting? Dear, dear, I am loth to let thee go."

"Don't fear for me, mother—I have the Governor's writing here, you know," said Ruth.

"Ah! but, cosset, the Governor's writing may not be worth a fig. He hath so belittled himself. Well, go, cosset—with God's blessing, go."

Without fear, Ruth stepped out of the narrow little entry into the brilliant sunlight. The hurry and excitement pleased her for a while, and covered the care in her heart. A tread too close to her own caused her to turn her head. Near by her side strode the Governor's secretary, with burning glance intent upon her. With a familiar "good-day," he walked confidently along, and whether she slackened or quickened her pace, he resolutely accompanied it.

"Let me carry thy burden, my pretty little maid," he said, holding forth his hand for the kettle; "thou art too lady-like for such servile business."

Ruth stopped, amazed.

"I do not know you, sir," she said.

"Don't know *me*, my dear? don't know the Governor's secretary? Why, yes; if thou choosest thou dost know me. Thou art a beautiful little maid—I have heard of thee—but of a surety the half hath not been told—no, nor the tenth part of thy sweet loveliness," he added, with a bold, admiring glance.

Ruth looked around, hoping to see some aid, but the crowd had passed, and the streets, save only the noise of distant shouts, were still.

"Will you let me go my way in peace?" asked Ruth, once more searching his face with her child-like, imploring gaze.

"Not in peace—unless—by heaven!" he said, stepping resolutely forward, "there is no one here; now just one kiss, my beauty—one kiss from those red lips! I do swear that thou art the brightest, the sweetest little maid! Come—"

He was in the act of passing his arm around the form of the shrinking girl, when a blow, dealt by a powerful hand, laid him senseless for the moment, and Ruth suddenly felt herself hurried along till a more public street was gained.

Not till he was leaving her did she see, through the disguise he had assumed, the eyes, the features, of Captain Cameron.

It pained her heart to think that he had not so much as spoken with her—that his look was stern, while his grasp upon her arm reminded her of that never-to-be-forgotten night at the tavern—and he was armed.

CHAPTER XVII.

THE INMATES OF THE JAIL.

THE men of Boston were roused to deeds of desperation. They swore at last to mob Government House, and make its inmates prisoners. Several personal friends of the Governor waited upon him. They found him moody, and chafing under the indignities he had lately felt, but only very recently understood.

"Your Excellency is not safe here," they said ; "you must go to the fort. The populace threatens."

"What! shall we make ourself a prisoner? No! by God's mercy, no!" was the defiant answer. "Let them come; we'll treat them to powder and shot."

"That's just what we wish to do," they replied. "For that reason we suggested the fort. There your Excellency has troops and cannon, and can soon put down this rebellion."

"By God's mercy! hath it reached that? Have the people taken up arms?"

The Governor grew pale. He remembered that the towns men had been wantonly provoked in too many cases.

"We regret to say that they have, Excellency," replied the spokesman ; "and we would take it upon ourselves to urge haste. Even now our movements may awaken suspicion. I hear they have taken solemn oath not to commence hostilities till to-morrow ; still, I depend not on them."

His secretary, in the mean time, being threatened, had taken refuge in the house of rector Aldrich, where, as the reader knows, Ruth was at present stopping.

He was made welcome with a Christian benevolence, though he was little liked. Ruth shrunk from his presence. As the evening prayer was ended, Captain Cameron came in. The secretary made feint to draw his sword, but the young ship-master only smiled as he said :

"I have no particular desire to save your life, which is worth but little at the best; but in consideration toward the ladies of this household, I give you fifteen minutes in which to reach the fort. If you do not avail yourself of this opportunity and my protection, the mob will be upon you, and I question if you will find any mercy at their hands. You may already hear their shouts bearing this way."

The secretary, as had the Governor, stood irresolute. Life was dear, and, as the young man had said, he had no reason to expect mercy at the hands of the people. Yet it was humiliating to be served thus, and he could not forbear his spite as he exclaimed :

"I like little to be indebted to a jail-bird for my life."

"No insinuations, if you please," said Captain Cameron, sternly. "Before many days pass, you, too, may pace the stone walls of a jail. It becomes not tenants of brittle houses to cast stones. I tell you to hurry, for the sake of the women," he added. "After the appointed time, even I can not save you."

"How do I know but you will deliver me into their hands?" asked the insolent secretary, changing color, as he heard the sounds of distant tumult.

"By the word of a man who never insulted an unprotected woman on the street," exclaimed Cameron, with an eye of fire, and moving steadily toward him.

"Ha! you are he who—" but he quailed before the incensed gaze of the ship-master, and, without wishing a good-night, or making a reverence, he stalked from the room.

Ruth's heart had been swelling with love, pride and grief, as, from her corner, she looked on during this conference. What was her astonishment when the young Captain, pausing at the door, said :

"By your leave, friends, I would speak with the maid Ruth a few moments, on my return."

"Certainly," said the minister, while Ruth's cheeks felt hot as she bore the scrutiny of the assemblage, and Lady Anne's direful glance filled her with dread.

———

The fort was situated on an eminence, called, in the old annals, Corn Hill. It was on one of the highest points of land overlooking the harbor—the islands, the ships that came

gallantly in from the open sea, and many of the neighboring
towns. It occupied the most prominent point on the hill.
There were two divisions: one called the lower, the other the
upper sconce, but both were connected by covered passages.
A few stately houses, built in the Elizabethan style of archi-
tecture, and surrounded by beautiful gardens, stood here and
there to the right and left of the fort. In these resided men
)f wealth and influence.

The fort was a substantial building, well provided with offi
cers, and securely palisaded. The artillery was of good force,
well mounted, and the particular pride of old gray-headed
Tony Butt, the gunner, who often declared, looking along the
circular front, that the harbor could be scoured the full
length of their shot on every side.

Here the Governor, compelled by circumstances over which
he had no control at present, breakfasted on the day after the
demonstration at his house. He had sent wary spies, since
daylight, to reconnoiter, but they invariably returned with
tidings not calculated to elevate the spirits of his Excellency or
the gentlemen who shared his durance vile. They reported
that the military were out, the people armed and gathering.
Fiercest denunciations were heaped upon the Governor, and
some of the townsmen were for executing instant vengeance.
His effigy had been made of straw, and was already on its
march through the streets, preparatory to being burnt on the
common. The river was filled with boats on the Charlestown
side, and the people there could be seen in crowds, waving
and shouting defiance.

"Would we could sink them," muttered the Governor.

Then came sounds of tumult—increasing, subsiding, again
seeming to approach, then to sink into comparative silence.

"Let the crows caw!" cried the secretary. "I shall enjoy
my coffee none the less. Come, gentlemen, we could hardly
have a better appointed breakfast even in a statelier mansion.
Yonder, see the bright eyes of Mistress Polly Colman; upon
my word, I do believe, had she the power, she would release
us. Come, gentlemen, don't let this little breeze ruffle your
appetites. We have friends in the town, surely, who will not
see us come to harm, whatever happens."

They drew up to the table. The Governor sipped his beverage with a clouded brow.

"His Excellency will bear in mind that I have endeavored to impress him with the importance of making an example of some of these leading rebels," said the secretary, shortly after. "For instance, had that dog of a Willie been shot, and that coward of a Captain hung, and two or three heads placed upon spikes before a window, the rabble townsmen might have been frightened into submission. His Excellency, in the great goodness of his heart, hath been too lenient."

"By mercy!" cried the Governor, frowning. "Dost throw blame on me?"

"By no means, Excellency—by no means. I was only thinking of a little feat that Jeffries managed—managed capitally! by Jove! There was a man among his party who showed symptoms of rebellion. A soldier's first duty is toward his superior officer. He had, I think, a wife—these common soldiers have no right to such luxuries—and a very beautiful daughter. The name of the latter was Eunice, and she was called the pretty Nice. Jeffries had before been suspicious of this man, (there goeth a pop-gun,) so when the pretty Nice came to the camp one day, and implored that her father might go and see his wife, who, mind thee, she pretended was ill and dying in a near town, Jeffries refused. That night the soldier and his daughter were found a mile from the town. He meant to go (so he said, mind thee,) and return by the morning.

"Well, as it was a clear case of desertion, he was brought before Jeffries, and, without a word, a shot was fired that found a warm bed in our soldier's heart. As for the daughter, the pretty Nice, (doctor, take a sandwich,) she never returned to her mother. Old Jeffries had an eye for fine girls—ha! ha! ha!"

The Governor pushed back his chair, his thoughts were still preoccupied. Some of the gentlemen smiled at the story, others frowned.

"I think we had best send a message for the ministers—they have great influence with the people," said the Governor, nervously. "What is the crowd, yonder?"

"They are forming a sort of guard," replied the secretary,

scanning the outposts. "To the guns. Order the soldiers to blow them to pieces."

Justice Bullivant arose. "That would be madness," he said, speaking hurriedly. "Before night the town would be over-run with the people from the country, and they would take a full vengeance. Boats-full are setting off from Charlestown now."

A soldier entered. The Captain of the frigate in the stream would send a boat to the rescue of his Excellency as soon as he could without exciting the suspicions of the people. Mean-while they were using all delay to get ready to sail.

"Then let us enjoy ourselves," said the secretary, with as-sumed courage, "and the first opportunity that occurs we will write this treachery in their blood—to perdition with 'em. Now, then, I'm ready to please you ; what shall it be, a song ? This is a fine thing—listen :

> " Come from thy rest, my lance !
>   Come from thy rest ;
> Strike where the white swords glance ;
>   Yon coward breast.
> Hark ! 'tis the battle-cry !
> Glory I'll win or die !
> Bannered by royal sky,
>   By valor blest.
>
> "Come to the field, my steed—
>   Come to the field ;
> Fly at the shout of need,
>   Scorn once to yield ;
> See, o'er the serried lines,
> Bronze-red the war-sun shines,
> Pouring his burning wines
>   On sword and shield.
>
> " Farewell all honey-sips,
>   Sweet Eoline ;
> Farewell thy ripened lips,
>   Thy voice divine ;
> If, 'mid the trumpet's din,
> One leaf of bay I win,
> Thy hand shall twine it in
>   These locks of mine.
>
> ' But, should a sadder note
>   Come tolling by,
> As wounded sparrows float,
>   Tremulously,
> Say, with thy lifted hand,
> 'God keep thee, Uldebrand !
> Who saveth Father-land,
>   Never can die !' "

" A right good scug I call that, and a spirited air too. One should hear the Lady Anne sing it; one should see her eye flash over it ! What a splendid soldier was lost in her lady-ship !"

" Did not the young poet, Ross, compose it ?" asked Justice Bullivant.

" Yes, when there was spirit in him, before he took to the pulpit, as they say he has—a fool ! What is there in these clarks and clergymen that takes the women so ? I have always seen how the maid Eleanor liked him," he added between his teeth.

" This is no time to talk of cooing and lovemating," said the Governor, turning from a narrow slip, through which he had been reconnoitering ; " but, by God's mercy, before our niece should marry that white-faced knave, we ourself would cleave his silly heart. Hark ! what is't the rebels say ?"

" They are shouting—they have captured the Captain and master of the frigate ; old Tony says they are dragging him into the town—that the frigate hath put out all her flags and pennants, and opened all her ports," said a soldier, from the outside.

" Thank God ! we have some friends, though they can not help us," said the Governor, with new energy.

Still another messenger arrived. The ministers all declined to come, he said—they did not think it safe for them, as the hearts of the people were bent on justice.

" Justice !" growled the Governor, pallid—grinding his teeth.

Thus, then, there seemed at present no possibility of escape. The star of freedom was in the ascendant. It shone with a faint, unequal light, destined soon to brighten all the horizon.

CHAPTER XVIII.

THE CONFESSIONAL AND ITS AGONY.

ONLY Ruth was left in the drawing-room, whose walls were gilded with dissolving though brilliant pictures, painted by the fitful fire on the hearth. Restlessly waiting and watching Ruth looked for the reappearance of young Cameron. Some one, on leaving the room, had playfully thrown a long blue silken scarf over her shoulders, and she had not removed it, for it was a novel thing to feel the light pressure of rich vestments. It formed a beautiful contrast to the pretty crimson merino, and certainly became her well. She looked, in that soft light, as if it was fitting for her to wear costly robes. A little maiden pride (and surely maid so beautiful never harbored less) had moved her to unloosen her bright tresses from their prim bandings. The locks thus falling did not exactly curl, but they fell in lustrous undulations, sweeping over her shoulders and mingling with the glistening fringe of the fair mantle. The fever of expectation gave a fervid rose-tint to either cheek, and her lips were brighter than usual.

It was quiet abroad. The old reverence for staid rules and particular hours did not break through the custom of the homeward path by nine. At every slight noise, however, Ruth's heart beat faster and louder—nor did its pulsations lessen as a wondering servant ushered in young Cameron. For a moment she stood, too much amazed to speak. He wore a long military cloak, which, when he threw it off, displayed a splendid uniform that made his beauty quite magnificent to a timid little Puritan maid like Ruth. The cap he laid on the table glittered with broad gold bands and a cockade, and from its sable summit hung gorgeous plumes of red and black.

"I am in borrowed feathers, Ruth," he said, gravely; "some of my fellow townsmen expressing a wish that I would equip myself in this suit, that belonged to his Excellency, out of good-humor I assented. This," he said, smiling, laying his hand upon the hilt, "is the secretary's sword. I trust I shall not disgrace the property of so gallant a gentleman," he added, with another smile. "And you, Ruth! what transforming touch has been busy with you? Why you look charmingly, my Ruth!"

She, blushing, essayed to throw aside the shining scarf, but he would not allow it, saying:

"We'll play at nabob for a while—'tis but nonsense, you know."

"Ruth, other lips have told you that you are very lovely," he continued, after gazing in her sweet, downcast face for a moment—a slumbering passion lying along his voice—"but not with the heart-intent that I say it. Oh! Ruth, I have had tormenting, maddening doubts. It seemed as if all who saw must covet you. I could not understand your penitence—for no guilt you had done—I can not comprehend that humility that others have praised in you—but, oh! Ruth, in spite of rumors—of the strange words that have fallen from your own lips—I love you—God, above, knows how dearly.

"And I come to-night, (he took her unresisting hand,) to hear from your dear lips all doubts removed, for they linger in spite of me. Oh! Ruth—love me to-night—let *me* love you as in the sunny time. To-morrow there may be bloodshed— and who knows but I may be the first to fall!"

With as pure a passion as man ever cherished, he held the trembling girl to his heart in a long, sweet fold, and, for the second time in her life, she rested there as if the rest were heaven.

"I know you will tell me all, Ruth; I am certain you can have no *sin* to confess," he added, looking down on her now pale face. "Come, my darling. Who has so sweet a right to know your heart's most precious secrets as I?"

"Yes, you have the right," murmured Ruth; "but (she looked up with that innocent, appealing look) it may cost me your love."

"Never, Ruth; my *love!* never, Ruth! You are more precious to me to-night than I can hope to tell you; don't fear me, darling."

"Do you remember, once, you told me you were proud?" she shuddered, pressing her hands upon her face, now crimson.

"Yes, Ruth—and I was proud; but, do you know, I have

never forgotten that saintly figure, standing so meek and white
at the head of the church aisle ? I tell you, Ruth, with all
my human revenge making my soul almost a hell, at that moment I thought of our blessed Savior, and you seemed to me
holy, like him."

"Oh ! no—no !"—Ruth shrunk away.

"Since then, in the darkness of my prison-nights, at noon-
day, wherever I have been, that vailed form has risen up before me, checked my passions, softened my rashness, rebuked
my pride. Oh! Ruth—your calm eyes ! your noble meekness
on that sacred morning, made me, I sometimes think, another
man. I did not see it then; but I do now. If I was proud
then, I have lost that kind of pride now, if I know myself.
Sit down, darling, you tremble."

He waited. Many times she opened her lips to speak, but
the words would not come. Perhaps if he had lost pride, she
had found it, for never did duty agonize her so. The dread
that he would be so shocked as to betray a feeling it was
hardly in the nature of man to suppress, kept her tongue
silent.

"My Ruth !"—he pushed the mantle aside, and the beaming
smile with which he regarded her made her courage falter the
more.

"Ruth—Ruth—are you afraid of me ?"

"No; oh! no—but it is hard to tell—to—" emotion checked
her voice; she could not proceed, but turned her face away.

"Listen, Ruth; to-morrow I shall be in deadly peril, if
things take the course for which they are shaped. But that
is not all, Ruth; if I escape then, I have still another dangerous duty to perform. I tell you these things, my darling, not
to make you suffer, but because I know you would not send
me from you, perhaps for the last time, feeling you had denied
me the confidence I have a right to claim—yes, a right," his
voice lingered fondly over the word. "A certain place in
the harbor is suspected. A gang of dangerous men, pirates,
Ruth, are living there, sheltered by the ghostly reputation of
the place. It is more than likely that among them are the
murderers and plunderers of whom the town authorities have
been in search. These men, since the apprehension of the
Governor, I have sworn to find—and thus, you see, danger

4

attends me for the present.   Ruth! Ruth!" (in a tone of consternation.)

She had grown paler and paler; now she turned toward
him with glassy eyes.

"The island!" she cried, brokenly; "then you may take
him—and, oh! he is already wounded—dying, perhaps. Captain—Captain Cameron," she cried, incoherently, her eyes still
painfully and glaringly distended, "you, yourself, have sealed
my lips. If I could not tell *then*, I *dare* not now. I must
not—interfere—with your sacred duty. And, if you know!—
justice must overtake them, (she clasped her hands wildly,)
and *then* you could not—oh! God help me!"   She sunk,
crouching, to the floor.

With knit brows and shut lips, Captain Cameron looked
down upon her.   Was the rumor—the fearful, maddening rumor, true?   Had he been doubly deceived?   The old, stormy
suspicion shook him from head to foot.

"You are only trying me, Ruth," and his voice shook with
his frame; "come—come—and tell me what you mean."

"Ask me nothing," Ruth said, lifting herself, growing suddenly strangely calm and cold.   "If you can believe my assertion that in no thing I am guil—"

The young man stamped his foot.

She dared neither speak nor move, his face was so fearful.

"One word! only one word!" he said, thickly.   "Answer
me yes or no, as you value your soul's eternal salvation.
Have you ever seen a man called by the people Captain Bill?
Either yes! or no! no more."

"Yes—I—"

"That will do—now, yes or no again—and *if* not *no*—God
have mercy on you!   Did you ever *meet* him at night?"

His steel-like glance was a horrible fascination.   She never
moved her fearful eyes from his face as she replied:

"I will tell you the truth; I have—but it was—"

"Silence!—Oh! my brain whirls!   Silence! open but
your lips, and—God knows whether my reason will hold!   It
was told me," he cried, striding in his hot wrath to the table
—clutching his cloak—his hat.   "Yes, and if it had been a
man had so insulted me by such suspicions, I should have run
him through.   As it was—I gave the lady the *lie!*   In spite

of her rank, I insolently answered her—'tis a lie! If she were here (he laughed bitterly) I would ask her pardon on my knees, as some gallants, they say, make love. Now, Ruth, farewell, forever ; never, never will I trust woman again."

———— ----

CHAPTER XIX.

THE GOVERNOR IN THE HANDS OF THE PEOPLE.

CAPTAIN CAMERON, with a few trusty men, had been on the search for the harbor-pirates, and was returning on the day after the Governor's incarceration, having found their place of retreat.

Stepping on Boston pier, he was hailed by friends on the watch for him.

"We were only waiting for you," said one, " to march to the fort. The declaration of an independence of Andros-rule was sent in to-day, and received with indignation and oaths. That bullying secretary even went so far as to return a contemptuous note to Governor Bradstreet, and it hath filled every honest heart with indignation."

The Governor, who had been watching uneasily at his accustomed window, felt some relief at sight of a messenger bearing a paper. He opened it eagerly, and, reading it through, with a fearful imprecation flung it to the ground, and was in the act of placing his heel upon it, when the soldier, with a quick movement, snatched it up.

"By God's mercy !" shouted the Governor, white with passion; " are they fools? Did not his Majesty send us? Have not the people confirmed us ? Is this honor? Is this allegiance ? Let them send us to England to receive our judgment there. We will not be held to account by the rabble. Go tell them, from us, that they are a pack of hell-hounds, and we will see them all hung before we do what they require."

"Your Excellency will allow me," said Justice Bullivant, very much agitated ; " we are prisoners, and therefore at the

mercy of the townspeople.   Had not your Excellency better
use more conciliatory language ?"

"Damn 'em !" muttered the secretary, as he walked to and
fro, and that was all he could say, for he had taken large
draughts of wine to fortify his failing courage.

"Conciliatory language !" returned the Governor; "read
for yourself," and he motioned the soldier to hand the note to
him.   It was thus couched :

"*At the Town House in Boston.*

"April 18th, 168—.

."To SIR EDMUND ANDROS—Sir : Ourselves and manie others, ye inhabitants of this towne and ye places adjacent, being
surprised at ye people's sudden taking up of arms, in ye first
motion whereof we were wholly ignorant, being driven by ye
present accident, are necessitated to acquaint your Excellency
that, for ye quieting and securing of ye people inhabiting in
this country from ye imminent dangers they manie ways lie
open and exposed to, and tendering your own safety, we
judge it necessary you forthwith surrender and deliver up ye
government and fortifications, to be preserved and disposed of
according to order and direction from ye crown of England,
w'h suddenly is expected may arrive, promising all security
from violence to yourself or anie of your gentlemen or soldiers
in person and estate ; otherwise we are assured they will endeavor the taking of ye fortification by storm if anie opposi-
tion be made."

To this document were signed fifteen names, that of the
venerable Bradstreet heading the list.

"I see not but this is very fair," said Bullivant, his hand
trembling so that the paper shook, for he did not want the
Governor to refuse.

"Fair !" shouted the Governor; " by God's mercy ! fair !
Shall we be made a laughing-stock by this accursed, low-born
commonalty ?   Tell the persons who sent that document that
we say *no !*" and rattling out his sword, he struck it flat-bladed
on the table before him.   The soldier hurried from the presence of this insulted dignitary, who, hot not only with passion
but with wine, poured forth volley after volley of curses and
reproaches—stamping, shaking his clenched hands, condensing
his passion into terrible eye-glances, with which he regarded

those about him, till even the half-drunken secretary seemed
ashamed of him.

The message was delivered, and excited the citizens to such
a degree that they were ready to storm the fort; some even
prepared chains and cords with which to bind the deposed
man. Governor Bradstreet, seeing the crowds congregated,
their furious gestures and and angry faces, conjured them in a
short speech not to do violence, but to let the news go to
England how courageous, firm, and yet generous they could
be. Every man looked capable of taking the lead, yet the
selection fell on Sir John Willie, who declined in favor of
Captain Cameron. He placed himself at their head, and thus,
silent but determined, they marched directly to the fort.

"So! the rebels are coming!" cried the Governor, his bra-
vado silenced.

"Oh! Excellency! the whole town is here," cried one of
the soldiers, almost beside himself with fear.

"And where are the men-at-arms—where are the men upon whom I depend for protection?"

"They are here, Excellency," returned the trembling soldier.

"What! in this building? By God's mercy—have they
not remained to give the rebels a broadside?"

"They did not have orders, Excellency; and—" the words
were stopped by a blow on the mouth from the enraged Governor, who proceeded to the door, and finding his men assembled, dealt them strokes right and left till they crowded
back and fled from his murderous weapon.

"They turn the guns upon us!" cried the secretary; "they
have possession of the fort. Will the wretches murder us in
cold blood?"

The Governor sunk on a seat. His frantic rage had spent
itself, and now came fear mixed with regrets. If the citizens
were in the mood, what would be easier than to shatter them
all to pieces? And he knew in his inmost heart that they had
been tortured into this rebellion. How ominous the silence
that followed! Only a low, murmuring whisper penetrated
the walls of the fort, until another messenger came. Captain
Cameron, with a quiet, gentlemanly dignity, presented himself.

"It is needless for me to say to you that the fort and

yourselves are in our possession," he said. "It is decided by a large majority, all ayes and no nays, that Sir Edmund Andros is no longer Governor-General of these Colonies. As a prisoner, then, I respectfully ask you to walk out with me. The townspeople are quite willing that, for the *present*, you should retire to a private dwelling-house, under a guard; but your secretary and the other"—he made a full pause—"and the gentlemen of your party," he added, "are to be lodged in jail."

Randolph turned toward him. His eyes glittered, snake-like—a whiteness mounted slowly from chin to brow, as he felt for his sword. It hung, however, by the side of Captain Cameron.

"It would be madness in one of you to resist," said the latter, quietly, returning the glare of the secretary so unflinch-ingly that the eye of the latter fell. "They stand by the guns outside, ready, on the slightest provocation, to let them blaze. Are you ready? I can not wait longer."

Utterly humiliated and crestfallen, the Governor, striving to collect himself, longing to perish by his own hand, but lacking the Roman hardihood to do the deed, equally unwil-ling to be blown to atoms, lifted himself from his seat, and striving to assume a lofty air, but utterly failing, he moved outside the fort. To their credit be it said, the townspeople did not triumph with wild huzzas over a fallen foe. With much decorum the military surrounded the Governor and his colleagues, a drum and fife were sounded, and thus they ac-companied the baffled tyrant to the place which had been assigned to him. There he was met by his friends.

Till toward night, the city seemed relapsing into its usual order. The officers and soldiers of the fort were under arrest —the streets were still. But the quiet was ominous, and des-tined soon to be broken into a wilder confusion than had yet reigned. By all the avenues leading to the country, bands of armed and angry men were marching into town. Every moment some new accession was made. Farmers, mechanics, tradesmen, doctors, soldiers, teachers, lawyers, harangued together. The substance of their cries and exclamations was that they wanted the Governor and would have him. In vain did the men in authority repeat their advice—their warning; all entreaty was wasted upon them. The crowds grew so clamorous that the whole city was in alarm.

"He is not safe enough where you have placed him. We must see him—we must chain him. He must go either to the fort or to the jail. Give us the Governor! the Governor!"

The mad cry went up appallingly—gaining in strength, swelling even to the ears of the fallen man. The bells were rung. Cannon thundered on the twilight air, and to the Governor's name were added the names of the Captain and master of the frigate Nothing would satisfy them, and as they surrounded the house, threatening to level it if the tyrant did not give himself into their hands, he was forced to appear, trembling now like a leaf, while his nieces uttered despairing cries.

The scene was fearful in the extreme. Shouts grew to howlings; excitement overruled reason. The war-spirit was in the ascendancy, and would vent itself in piercing sounds and lawless tumults.

"I fear we shall have trouble in earnest," said the schoolmaster, stopping a moment by the side of Sir John Willie, who looked on uneasily, having no influence over this outbreak.

"It looks so!" said the young man. "See! they are tying his hands—oh! shame! I like it not," he added, with indignant emphasis, a glow of mortification mantling his cheeks.

At that moment, a man, athletic and middle-aged, stepped out from the crowd. His manner riveted attention, much more his startling voice, his determined gestures, as he yelled:

"Give the prisoner into my hands, gentlemen. Two years ago, this devil caused my father to be falsely imprisoned in England. Falsely—mark! The poor old man laid his white hairs upon the stone floor, and there died of grief. 'Tis not the only one he has done to death—the slow murder of a poor, helpless, old, gray-haired woman this very month, in yonder jail, calls for vengeance. Now *I* wish to have the *pleasure* of taking this ex-Governor by the collar of his coat, as I would take a beast by its halter, and leading him to jail."

Up went an exultant shout.

"To the fort, rather," cried several voices.

"Very well, to the fort, and after that to the jail!" cried the athletic man, taking the Governor, with a rude jerk, by the collar. Thus, with jeers and derision, was he led along.

The work was not yet finished. Returning after the safer deposit of the ex-Governor, they demanded the Captain of the frigate. He was brought from the Red Lion, a woe-begone image—expecting insult, perhaps death.

."He must surrender his ship," shouted some one.

This was even worse than death to the Captain.

"Gentlemen! gentlemen!" he cried, "don't deprive us of our wages; ask any concession, and I'm bound to do your will and sail off as soon as possible for England."

"We'll give you better wages," they shouted. "Hurrah for the British Captain who don't want to lose his wages!"

"Go strike your topmasts and bring the sails ashore," said Captain Cameron.

"Good!" cried the multitude, and hurried to send the Captain to his ship. This action diverted their minds, and made them better-natured.

In a short time the Captain, well guarded, was on board his vessel, actively giving directions, and very soon the people on shore had the pleasure of handling the abstracted sails, and of seeing that their orders were fully obeyed.

In the mean time many a fugitive had been diligently hunted up. Young men scoured the country far and near and where they found any one who had taken measures with the Government, he was forthwith imprisoned.

The Governor's house had been thoroughly ransacked, his carriage rendered useless, his horses appropriated, and every thing belonging to him treated with contempt. His Excellency was led out of the fort on another forced march, and left, finally, within the odious jail-walls, his glory all departed.

Not long could Cameron remain inactive. He determined, therefore, to busy himself about the capture of the pirates. He had, accordingly, procured an armed force, and all things were prepared with the greatest secrecy, so as to surprise and overpower the murderers and their abettors. The young man was restless, and had grown pale with loss of sleep, but he could not allow himself to be idle for a moment.

His hands were full—he could not be idle if he would. There was his ship to superintend, hands to find to man her, and cargoes for her lading. So he allowed himself no time to think. Only when the curtain of the night fell over him, that one face—that sweet, white, pleading face, was ever before him and would not let him sleep.

And how fared it with Ruth ?

Well!

The trial of her faith and love had not left the maid either despairing or desponding.

CHAPTER XX.

RUTH VINDICATED AT LAST.

A TERRIBLE disease had broken out in the minister's family, and Ruth was sent back to the Red Lion, to escape infection. Captain Cameron had gone down the harbor to capture the pirates lurking about the islands. Mistress Bean received Ruth kindly, and seemed anxious to forget the past. But, Ruth could not sit down and chat with her as she wished— firing whole volleys of questions as to the circumstances, habits, temper and means of the "Episcopals."

"And isn't it dreadful," she said, " to think that the poor creatures are afflicted so ? Well, well ; what strange things happen ! Here's the Governor in prison with his fine-dressed secretary ; father Comstock, poor man, sick in his bed from fatigue and worry ; and Cameron gone after pirates. Didst ever see such a come-together state of affairs ?"

Ruth had no heart to answer. The long day dragged wearily away, and toward evening, as she stood at a window looking upon the street, she gave a low, painful cry, that startled the widow and brought her to her side.

"Mercy deliver us, child ! What hath happened ? Two

men stretched out. Pray God one may not be the Captain !''

" But it is ! it is !'' moaned Ruth.

" And those horrible creatures ! They must be the pirates!
How the soldiers watch them ! Well, they stop here. The
poor Captain !   But I had rather they went elsewhere.''

" You will send him away !'' cried Ruth, hollowly, laying
her hand on the widow's arm.

" Why child ! I have a heart—and—but here cometh the
chambermaid. Two beds ! get thee two beds ready,'' said
Mistress Bean, hastily, " and put them both in the large chamber leading from the first flight. Is he badly hurt, Temper-
ance ?''

" They say they can't tell, ma'am,'' replied the girl ; " they've
sent after a doctor ;'' and away she hurried.

" Come with us, child,'' said the widow ; and Ruth, striving
to calm herself, followed her foster-mother. They entered the
room as some one was placing the body of Captain Cameron
on a bed. He was very faint and helpless, and over one arm
he had no control whatever. He saw Ruth standing with her
troubled eyes fixed upon him. He shuddered as he met her
gaze, and turned his face to the wall. The sight of her
seemed to give him pain.

In a few moments the other body was brought in. It was
but a body, for, as they laid it on a bed, one of the men exclaimed, " he's done breathing. I thought he couldn't last to
get here.''

Ruth was looking on, her hands tightly clasped. She
caught sight of the rigid features of the dead—and with a loud,
heart-rending cry of " My poor, poor, father !'' stood sobbing
at the bedside of the corpse.

" Oh ! you *have* suffered—you *have* suffered,'' she murmured,
kneeling and scanning closely the worn and channeled face.
" This, this is sorrow !—to know what he was ! and to see
him thus !'' Sobbing, she buried her head in her hands.

" That beats all,'' said one of the men ; " this here must be
the old pirate Blunderbuss Hal !'' while Captain Cameron, under the influence of strong feeling, had raised himself in bed,
and. clutching at the edge to keep himself upright, was looking on in wild amaze.

At last he sunk back heavily. The men, respecting Ruth's grief, left the chamber, telling each other that strange things happened; for they had supposed Blunderbuss Hal dead, long ago—and so had everybody else.

"Ruth," cried Captain Cameron, in weak tones.

She came slowly toward him, and falling by his bed, still kept her face in her hands.

"Ruth—is this so? Ruth—have I been thus unjust to you? My poor Ruth—God forgive me if I have! I see now—you are a noble girl, Ruth Margerie!"

"I can tell you now," she said, in a voice full of sad music, as by a strong effort she checked her tears. "It was my poor father I met on that first night, and who kissed me. He exacted a solemn promise from me, that I would not let a living soul know that he was on the coast. He said that many thought him lost, and if they knew he was still living they would hunt him to the death, for there was a price set on his head. I was frightened, and repeated the words of an oath after him—and then—how could I tell? For his sake I have borne (her voice faltered) what, perhaps, I could not bear again—but oh! the hardest of all was the loss of your confidence."

"Noble Ruth Margerie! Noble Ruth Margerie!" said the self-convicted man—and he tried to place his hand upon her head, but could not.

"He promised me that he had done with evil deeds, and if he might only be confided in by me, it would help him to be a better man. So, though I shrunk from him—I could not help it—he kissed me;—he was *my father*, you know."

"Blessed Ruth!" murmured Captain Cameron.

"And it seemed to me that I might save him," she continued, sobbing a little—"oh! I thought how glorious it would be—worth bearing all my humiliations for—oh yes, much more! And I prayed for him night and day; and when I stood there, before all the people, I seemed to hear a voice whispering to me, "it is not all in vain, Ruth," and it made me happy—so happy!"

"But, when I was called again—I did not see him—but—that other—that dreadful Captain Bill—and from him I learned what I would not have dreamed, otherwise, that my poor,

guilty father—had once more stained his hands with blood.
Oh ! this—this was hard to bear !"

"Yes ! and if you had gone with him, Ruth ? I have had
a fearful plot revealed to me. You would never have seen
your father. Their piratical vessel lays miles from here, where
no human ear could have heard your cries. Great God, I
thank thee !"

He wiped the crowding dew from his forehead with his free
hand. The intense excitement greatly prostrated the wounded
man. He struggled with his pain, and yet, through it all,
seemed happy in the consciousness of the great cloud having
passed away.

"The ball entered my side—and I can not tell—whether it is
fatal, though—I fear it. They are coming—stay by me—stay
by me, till the last, Ruth."

The doctor and several gentlemen came in. Their expressive silence and concerned looks spoke more eloquently than
words. Sir John Willie rendered all the assistance that was
needed.

The ball was extracted—one sharp cry of pain had gone to
Ruth's heart—then they sent the half-fainting girl for lint and
water.

CHAPTER XXI.

TWO LETTERS FROM A BRITISH MERCHANT TO HIS WIFE.

"My Darling :—As I was getting ready to have my luggage
placed on board the 'Prudent Sarah,' news came to me that
the master was desperate wounded, and so, of course, the
matter had to be put off for the present.

"That was four weeks ago, during w'h time I have been off
far in the country, prospecting, and only returned two days
ago so fatigued that I could not put pen to paper before. Well
—thou hast been informed, though I am not sure that the information has reached thee yet—that the Governor and his
companie are still in the jail. I have been to see his Excellency, and he is very much changed—quite submissive. I

can not help thinking the people have acted out their honest convictions, and I should not be surprised if at some future time the Colonies should rule themselves.   There is wide water between the two lands, which adds to making it probable. The young Captain is now recovering, and handsomer than ever.   Captain Bill, the notorious pirate, hath made horrible confession.   It seems that for years he has loved the maid Ruth, and pursued his unholy business that he might have wealth enough to take her to a foreign land, after he had entrapped her.   They keep him safe in irons, for even in confinement he is a dangerous man.

"And I do so hate to tell thee ! and at the same time delight to tell thee—for now all the mysterie is cleared up and Ruth acquitted.   Still, it hath come to light that a dreadful pirate, who died lately, was her own father.   To be sure she has had nothing to do with him these ten years—knew not, till now, that he was in the land of the living—and, as many another, till quite recent time, considered him dead.   And she so different ! so slight ! graceful and lady-like !   I can hardly comprehend it.   Thou wouldst not think her low-born ; no, not even for a moment.

"The news of the towne may not be uninteresting to thee. The old officers of Government of 1686 have assumed a sort of conservative control, until news shall be received from England."

(SECOND LETTER.)

"Three days later:

"It seems very laughable when I think that mayhap many of my last letters will go with me, and thou wilt have the pleasure of reading the same with me, meekly sitting as thine opposite.   I have every day new astonishments and new surprises, so that if I do not make haste to go from this enchanted land, I know not what will happen to myself.   And I am verie sure I have told thee nothing quite so strange as that I have to tell thee on this sheet.

"It seemeth, then, that a noble lady now in this Colony, Lady Bellamont, by reason of a visitation from God, (small-pox—I dared not tell thee till the danger was over,) hath been brought to her right senses, and made a strange and terrible confession. She, in her youth—then a noble lady--loved young Aldrich

who was a commoner.   When she saw another preferred before her, she offered herself, with wealth and title, to him, but
he refused, and almost despised her for the act.   Then her
love turned to hate, and she studied but for revenge.   It seems
that she stole two children from the minister some years after,
and brought them to America.   One of them proves to be
Captain Cameron, (who has been her especial *protégé*); the
other—now hold thy breath—the Lady Alicia Montrose—otherwise, little Ruth Margerie!   Think of that!   The little maid
was taken by the rector and his wife after the abduction of
their son, on account of her great loss, she having been deprived of both parents by a pestilence.   While the poor little
girl was being conveyed from her adopted home, on shipboard,
to this country, a poor woman lost her babe, a little girl.
This wicked abductor immediately gave little Lady Alice
to the poor creature.   The woman was the wife of a sailor
who had committed some crime for which he had to fly.
Subsequently he became a terrible pirate, and was known as
'Red Hand of Boston Bay.'   He never knew that his own
child was lost, and of course, to him, the little Ruth (so the
woman called her) was as his daughter.   There! if that is
not a romance for these new Colonies, what shall I give
you ?

  "I know not that I could describe the wedding.

  "'Wedding!' criest thou.

  "Yea, verily !   The Lady Bellamont hath made the young
Captain Cameron her heir, so that he had fit fortune to be
married with.   In consequence they had a great time at the
house of—the reverend Cotton Mather.   He desired and insisted that the wedding should be there—and it was also
Ruth's choice (I must call her by that sweet pretty name,)
Ah ! and such a companie as was gathered !—the very best of
the land.   And Cotton Mather was never so jollie and jovial.
The bride was dressed—(can I remember ?)—in satin and
pearls, I think—family-pearls, very beautiful !   The saintlie
look she hath not lost—but I think it rather gained on her.
Oh ! thou wilt love her dearly when thou knowest her, as I
mean thou shalt.

  "Among the companie were all that I have before spoken
to thee about.   Sir Edmund's two nieces and the gentlemen to

whom they will be married as soon as affairs are better settled
—all the humble folk, also, whom Ruth hath been among.

"The good old father Comstock, of whose fiddling and psalm-
ody I wrote thee, was not able to be there on account of ill-
ness, from w'h he will likely never recover. He is a good old
man. Schoolmaster Gamaliel Whiting—yea—and the phthis-
icky old schoolmistress and her opposite—in a word, the parlors
and all the rooms were full.

"Meantime the Governor hath nearly made his escape
twice—but he is at present in durance vile, with his secretary.
The poor, miserable pirate, when told how affairs were, took
sullen and lost all hope. He hath not spoken since. He will
now be sent to England to be hung.

"And now, on parting, let me tell thee (parting with my
pen) that we two must surelie return and live in this pleasant
countrie—far pleasanter in many respects than even England,
w'h, believe me, thou wilt not long regret.

"I do not think there is a happier couple in the wide world
than Captain Aldrich and his beautiful wife, whom he still
persisteth in calling Ruth.

"So, my darling, no more at present—from thy

LAMB."

THE END.

GEORGE ROUTLEDGE & SONS'
RAILWAY CATALOGUE.

. *The columns of prices show the forms in which the Books are kept —e.g., Ainsworth's Novels are kept only in paper covers at 1/, or limp cloth gilt, 1/6; Armstrong's only in picture boards at 2/, or half roan 2/6.*

Paper Covers.	Limp Cl. Gilt.					Picture Boards.	Hf. Roan.
		AINSWORTH, W. Harrison—					
1/	1/6	Auriol				—	—
1/	1/6	Crichton				—	—
1/	1/6	Flitch of Bacon				—	—
1/	1/6	Guy Fawkes				—	—
1/	1/6	Jack Sheppard				—	—
1/	1/6	James the Second				—	—
1/	1/6	Lancashire Witches				—	—
1/	1/6	Mervyn Clitheroe				—	—
1/	1/6	Miser's Daughter...				—	—
1/	1/6	Old St. Paul's				—	—
1/	1/6	Ovingdean Grange				—	—
1/	1/6	Rookwood...				—	—
1/	1/6	Spendthrift				—	—
1/	1/6	Star Chamber				—	—
1/	1/6	St. James'...				—	—
1/	1/6	Tower of London				—	—
1/	1/6	Windsor Castle				—	—

Ainsworth's Novels, in 17 vols., paper covers, price 17s.; cloth gilt, £1 5s. 6d.; 8 vols., half roan, £1 5s

		ALCOTT, Louisa M.—					
1/	2/	Little Women				—	—
1/	2/	Little Women Married				—	—
1/	1/6	Moods				—	—

		ARMSTRONG, F. C.—					
—	—	Medora				2/	2/6
—	—	The Two Midshipmen				2/	2/6
—	—	War Hawk				2/	2/6
—	—	Young Commodore				2/	2/6

The Set, in 4 vols., cloth, 10s.; or boards, 8s.

Paper Covers.	Limp Cl. Gilt.		Picture Boards.	
		ARTHUR, T. S.—		
1/	1/6	Nothing but Money	—	—
		AUSTEN, Jane—		Cloth.
1/	1/6	Emma	—	2/
1/	1/6	Mansfield Park	—	2/
1/	1/6	Northanger Abbey and Persuasion	—	2/
1/	1/6	Pride and Prejudice	—	2/
1/	1/6	Sense and Sensibility	—	2/

Jane Austen's Novels, 5 vols., paper covers, 5s.; cloth, 7s. 6d.; Superior Edition, cloth, in a box, 10s.

Paper Covers.	Limp Cl. Gilt.		Picture Boards.	
		BALZAC—		
1/	—	Balthazar	—	—
1/	—	Eugenie Grandet	—	—
		BANIM, John—		Hf. Roan.
—	—	Peep o' Day 2/	2/6	
—	—	Smuggler 2/	2/6	
		BARHAM, R. H.—		
1/	—	My Cousin Nicholas	—	—
		BAYLY, T. Haynes—		
1/	1/6	Kindness in Women	—	—
		BELL, M. M.—		
—	—	Deeds, not Words 2/	2/6	
—	—	The Ladder of Gold 2/	2/6	
—	—	The Secret of a Life 2/	2/6	
		BIRD, Robert M.—		
—	—	Nick of the Woods; or, The Fighting Quaker 2/	—	
		BRET HARTE—		
		See " AMERICAN LIBRARY," page 23.		
		BROTHERTON, Mrs.—		
1/	1/6	Respectable Sinners	—	—
		BRUNTON, Mrs.—		
1/	—	Discipline	—	—
1/	—	Self Control	—	—
		BURY, Lady Charlotte—		
1/	—	The Divorced	—	—
1/	—	Love	—	—

Paper Covers.	Limp Cl. Gilt.		Picture Boards.	Hf. Roan.
		CARLETON, William—		
1/	1/6	Clarionet, &c.	—	—
1/	1/6	Emigrants	—	—
1/	1/6	Fardarougha the Miser	—	—
1/	1/6	Jane Sinclair, &c.	—	—
1/	1/6	Tithe Proctor	—	—

Carleton's Novels, 5 vols., paper covers, 5s.; cloth, 7s. 6d.

		CHAMIER, Captain—		
—	—	Ben Brace	2/	2/6
—	—	Jack Adams	2/	2/6
—	—	Life of a Sailor	2/	2/6
—	—	Tom Bowling	2/	2/6

Chamier's Novels, 4 vols., bds., 8s.; cloth, 10s.

		CLARKE, M. C.—		
—	—	The Iron Cousin	2/	—

		COCKTON, Henry—		
—	—	George Julian, the Prince ...	2/	2/6
—	—	Stanley Thorn	2/	2/6
—	—	Valentine Vox, the Ventriloquist	2/	2/6

Cockton's Novels, 3 vols., boards, 6s.; half roan, 7s. 6d.

		COLLINS, Charles Alston—		
—	—	A Cruise upon Wheels ...	2/	—

COOPER, J. Fenimore—

(SIXPENNY EDITION *on page* 20.)

Paper Covers.	Limp Cl. Gilt.		Cl. Boards Gilt. with Frontispiece	
1/	1/6	Afloat and Ashore ; a Sequel to Miles Wallingford	2/	2/6
1/	1/6	Borderers ; or, The Heathcotes...	2/	2/6
1/	1/6	Bravo ; a Tale of Venice ...	2/	2/6
1/	1/6	Deerslayer ; or, The First War-Path	2/	2/6
1/	1/6	Eve Effingham : A Sequel to "Homeward Bound"	—	—
1/	1/6	Headsman...	2/	2/6
1/	1/6	Heidenmauer : a Legend of the Rhine	2/	2/6
1/	1/6	Homeward Bound ; or, The Chase	2/	2/6
1/	1/6	Last of the Mohicans	2/	2/6
1/	1/6	Lionel Lincoln ; or, The Leaguer of Boston	2/	2/6
1/	1/6	Mark's Reef ; or, The Crater ...	—	—

Paper Covers.	Limp Cl. Gilt.		Picture Boards.	Cl. Gilt, with Frontis- piece.
		COOPER, J. FENIMORE—*continued.*		
1/	1/6	Miles Wallingford; or, Lucy Hardinge	2/	2/6
1/	1/6	Ned Myers; or, Life before the Mast	—	—
1/	1/6	Oak Openings; or, The Beehunter	—	—
1/	1/6	Pathfinder; or, The Inland Sea	2/	2/6
1/	1/6	Pilot : a Tale of the Sea ...	2/	2/6
1/	1/6	Pioneers; or, The Sources of the Susquehanna	2/	2/6
1/	1/6	Prairie	2/	2/6
1/	1/6	Precaution	—	—
1/	1/6	Red Rover	2/	2/6
1/	1/6	Satanstoe; or, The Littlepage Manuscripts	—	—
1/	1/6	Sea Lions; or, The Lost Sealers	—	—
1/	1/6	Spy : a Tale of the Neutral Ground	2/	2/6
1/	1/6	Two Admirals	—	—
1/	1/6	Waterwitch; or, The Skimmer of the Seas...	2/	2/6
1/	1/6	Wyandotte; or, The Hutted Knoll	2/	2/6

Cooper's Novels.—The Set of 18 vols., green cloth, £2 5*s.*; boards, £1 16*s.*

The SHILLING EDITION, 26 vols. in 13, cloth, £1 19*s.* Also 26 vols., cloth gilt, £1 19*s.*; paper covers, £1 6*s.*

See also page 20.

		COOPER, Thomas—		Hf. Roan.
1/	1/6	The Family Feud	—	—
		COSTELLO, Dudley—		
—	—	Faint Heart ne'er Won Fair Lady	2/	—
—	—	The Millionaire of Mincing Lane	2/	—
		CROLY, Rev. Dr.—		
—	—	Salathiel	2/	2/6
		CROWE, Catherine—		
—	—	Lilly Dawson	2/	2/6
—	—	Linny Lockwood...	2/	2/6
—	—	Night Side of Nature	2/	2/6
—	—	Susan Hopley	2/	2/6
		The Set, 4 vols., cloth, 10*s.*		

RAILWAY CATALOGUE.

Paper Covers.	Limp Cl. Gilt.		Picture Boards.	Cloth or Hf. Roan.
		CROWQUILL, Alfred—		
1/	—	A Bundle of Crowquills	—	—
		CUMMINS, M. S.—		Cloth.
1/	1/6	The Lamplighter...	2/	2/6
—	—	Mabel Vaughan	2/	2/6
		CUPPLES, Captain—		Hf. Roan.
—	—	The Green Hand	2/	2/6
—	—	The Two Frigates	2/	2/6
		DE VIGNY, A.—		
1/	1/6	Cinq Mars	—	—
		DUMAS, Alexandre—		
1/	1/6	Ascanio	—	—
1/	1/6	Beau Tancrede	—	—
1/	1/6	Black Tulip	—	—
1/	1/6	Captain Paul	—	—
1/	1/6	Catherine Blum	—	—
1/	1/6	Chevalier de Maison Rouge ...	—	—
1/	1/6	Chicot the Jester	—	—
1/	1/6	Conspirators	—	—
1/	1/6	Countess de Charny	—	—
1/	1/6	Dr. Basilius	—	—
1/	1/6	Forty-five Guardsmen	—	—
—	—	Half Brothers	2/	2/6
1/	1/6	Ingenue	—	—
1/	1/6	Isabel of Bavaria	—	—
—	—	Marguerite de Valois	2/	2/6
1/	1/6	Memoirs of a Physician, vol. 1 }	—	3/
1/	1/6	Do. do. vol. 2 }		
1/	1/6	Monte Cristo ... vol. 1 }	—	3/
1/	1/6	Do. ... vol. 2 }		
1/	1/6	Nanon	—	—
1/	1/6	Page of the Duke of Savoy ...	—	—
1/	1/6	Pauline	—	—
1/	1/6	Queen's Necklace	—	—
1/	1/6	Regent's Daughter	—	—
1/	1/6	Russian Gipsy	—	—
1/	1/6	Taking the Bastile, vol. 1 }	—	3/
1/	1/6	Do. vol. 2 }		
1/	1/6	Three Musketeers ... }	—	3/
1/	1/6	Twenty Years After ... }		

Paper Covers.	Limp CL Gilt.					Picture Boards.	Hf. Roan.
		DUMAS, ALEXANDRE—*continued.*					
1/	1/6	Twin Captains	...	...	...	—	—
1/	1/6	Two Dianas	...	...	...	—	—
—	—	Vicomte de Bragelonne, vol. 1		...		2/6	3/
—	—	Do. do. vol. 2		...		2/6	3/
1/	1/6	Watchmaker	...	...	...	—	—

Dumas' Novels, 18 vols., half roan, £2 13s.

EDGEWORTH, Maria—

TALES OF FASHIONABLE LIFE :

1/	—	The Absentee ...	...	...		—	—
1/	—	Ennui ...	...	...	...	—	—
1/	—	Manœuvring	...	...	...	—	—
1/	—	Vivian ...	...	...	...	—	—

The Set, in cloth gilt, 4 vols., in a box, 8s.

EDWARDS, Amelia B.—

—	—	Half a Million of Money...		...		2/	2/6
—	—	Ladder of Life ...		...	...	2/	2/6
—	—	My Brother's Wife		...	...	2/	2/6

The Set, 3 vols., half roan, 7s. 6d.

FERRIER, Miss—

—	—	Destiny ...	...	...	...	2/	2/6
—	—	Inheritance	...	...	...	2/	2/6
—	—	Marriage ...	...	...	...	2/	2/6

The Set, 3 vols., half roan, 7s. 6d. ; in boards, 6s.

FIELDING, Thomas—

—	—	Amelia ...	...	...	...	2/	2/6
—	—	Joseph Andrews ...		...	...	2/	2/6
1/	—	Tom Jones	...	...	...	2/	2/6

Fielding's Novels, 3 vols., half roan, 7s. 6d. ; boards, 6s.
See also page 21.

FITTIS, Robert S.—

—	—	Gildcroy ...	...	...	...	2/	2/6

Paper Covers.	Limp Cl. Gilt.		Picture Cards.	Hf. Roan.
		FONBLANQUE, Albany, Jun.—		
—	—	The Man of Fortune	2/	2 6
		GERSTAECKER, Fred.—		
—	—	Each for Himself...	2/	2 6
—	—	The Feathered Arrow	2/	2 6
—	—	Sailor's Adventures		
—	—	The Haunted House }	2/	2 6
—	—	Pirates of the Mississippi ...	2/	2 6
—	—	Two Convicts	2/	2 6
—	—	Wife to Order	2/	2 6
		The Set, 6 vols., half roan, 15s.		
		GRANT, James—		Hf. Roan.
—	—	Aide de Camp	2/	2 6
—	—	Arthur Blane; or, The Hundred Cuirassiers	2/	2 6
—	—	Bothwell: the Days of Mary Queen of Scots...	2/	2 6
—	—	Captain of the Guard: the Times of James II.	2/	2 6
—	—	Cavaliers of Fortune; or, British Heroes in Foreign Wars ...	2/	2 6
—	—	Constable of France	2/	2 6
—	—	Dick Rodney: Adventures of an Eton Boy	2/	2 6
—	—	First Love and Last Love: a Tale of the Indian Mutiny	2/	2 6
—	—	Frank Hilton; or, The Queen's Own	2/	2 6
—	—	The Girl he Married: Scenes in the Life of a Scotch Laird ...	2/	2 6
—	—	Harry Ogilvie; or, The Black Dragoons	2/	2 6
—	—	Jack Manly	2/	2 6
—	—	Jane Seton; or, The King's Advocate	2/	2 6
—	—	King's Own Borderers; or, 25th Regiment	2/	2/6
—	—	Lady Wedderburn's Wish: a Story of the Crimean War	2/	2/6
—	—	Laura Everingham; or, The Highlanders of Glen Ora	2/	2/6
—	—	Legends of the Black Watch; or, The 42nd Regiment	2/	2/6

Paper Covers.	Limp Cl. Gilt.		Picture Boards.	Half Roan.

GRANT, JAMES—*continued.*

			Picture Boards	Half Roan
—	—	Lucy Arden ; or, Hollywood Hall	2/	2/6
—	—	Letty Hyde's Lovers : a Tale of the Household Brigade ...	2/	2/6
—	—	Mary of Lorraine...	2/	2/6
—	—	Oliver Ellis : the Twenty-first Fusiliers	2/	2/6
—	—	Only an Ensign	2/	2/6
—	—	Phantom Regiment : Stories of " Ours "...	2/	2/6
—	—	Philip Rollo ; or, The Scottish Musketeers	2/	2/6
—	—	Rob Roy, Adventures of ...	2/	2/6
—	—	Romance of War ; or, The Highlanders in Spain	2/	2/6
—	—	Scottish Cavalier : a Tale of the Revolution of 1688	2/	2/6
—	—	Second to None ; or, The Scots Greys	2/	2/6
—	—	Under the Red Dragon	2/	2/6
—	—	White Cockade ; or, Faith and Fortitude	2/	2/6
—	—	Yellow Frigate	2/	2/6

James Grant's Novels, 31 vols., half roan, £3 17s. 6d. ; boards, £3 2s.

GLEIG, G. R.—

				Hf. Roan.
—	—	The Country Curate	2/	2/6
—	—	The Hussar	2/	2/6
—	—	Light Dragoon	2/	2/6
—	—	The Only Daughter	2/	2/6
—	—	The Veterans of Chelsea Hospital	2/	2/6
—	—	Waltham	2/	2/6

The Set in 6 vols., half roan, 15s.

GOLDSMITH, Oliver—

1/	—	The Vicar of Wakefield	—	—

GRIFFIN, Gerald—

1/	1/6	Colleen Bawn	—	—
1/	1/6	Munster Festivals...	—	—
1/	1/6	The Rivals	—	—

Griffin's Novels, 3 vols., cloth, 4s. 6d. ; paper, 3s.

Paper Covers	Limp Cl. Gilt		Picture Boards.	Hf. Roan.
		GORE, Mrs.—		
—	—	Cecil	2/	2 6
—	—	Debutante	2/	2 6
—	—	The Dowager ... `	2/	2 6
—	—	Heir of Selwood	2/	2 6
—	—	Money Lender	2/	2 6
—	—	Mothers and Daughters	2/	2 6
—	—	Pin Money	2/	2 6
—	—	Self	2/	2,6
—	—	The Soldier of Lyons	2/	2/6

The Set, 9 vols., half roan, £1 2s. 6d.

		GREY, Mrs.—		
1/	1/6	The Duke	—	—
1/	1/6	The Little Wife	—	—
1/	1/6	Old Country House	—	—
1/	1/6	Young Prima Donna	—	—

The Set, in 4 vols., 6s., cloth gilt.

		HALIBURTON, Judge—		
—	—	The Attaché	2/	2/6
—	—	The Letter-Bag of the Great Western	2/	2/6
—	—	Sam Slick, the Clockmaker ...	2/6	3/

Haliburton's Novels, 3 vols., half roan, 8s.; paper covers, or boards, 6s. 6d.

		HANNAY, James—		
—	—	Singleton Fontenoy	2/	—

		HARLAND, Marion—		
1/	—	Hidden Path	—	—

HARTE, Bret—

See page 23.

		HAWTHORNE, Nathaniel—		
1/	1/6	The House of the Seven Gables ..	—	—
1/	1/6	Mosses from an Old Manse ...	—	—
1/	1/6	The Scarlet Letter	—	—

		HEYSE, Paul (Translated by G. H. Kingsley)—		
1/	—	Love Tales	—	—

Paper Covers.	Limp Cl. Gilt.		Picture Boards.	Hf. Roan.

HOOD, Thomas—

—	—	Tylney Hall	2/	2/6

HOOK, Theodore—

—	—	All in the Wrong...	2/	2/6
—	—	Cousin Geoffry	2/	2/6
—	—	Cousin William	2/	2/6
—	—	Fathers and Sons...	2/	2/6
—	—	Gervase Skinner	2/	2/6
—.	--	Gilbert Gurney	2/	2/6
—	—	Gurney Married	2/	2/6
—	—	Jack Brag	2/	2/6
—	—	The Man of Many Friends ...	2/	2/6
—	--	Maxwell	2/	2/6
—	—	Merton	2/	2/6
—	—	Parson's Daughter	2/	2/6
—	—	Passion and Principle	2/	2/6
—	—	Peregrine Bunce	2/	2/6
—	—	The Widow and the Marquess ...	2/	2/6

Hook's Novels, 15 vols., half roan, £2; Sayings and Doings, 5 vols., half roan, 12s. 6d.

JAMES, G. P. R.—

—	—	Agincourt	2/	—
—	—	Arabella Stuart	2/	—
—	—	Black Eagle	2/	—
—	—	The Brigand	2/	—
—	—	Castle of Ehrenstein	2/	—
—	—	The Convict	2/	—
—	—	Darnley	2/	—
—	—	Forgery	2/	—
—	—	The Gentleman of the Old School	2/	—
—	—	The Gipsy	2/	—
—	—	Gowrie	2/	—
—	—	Heidelberg	2/	—
—	—	Jacquerie	2/	—
—	—	Morley Ernstein	2/	—
—	—	Philip Augustus	2/	—
—	—	Richelieu	2/	—
—	—	The Robber	2/	—
—	—	Russell	2/	—
—	—	The Smuggler	2/	—
—	—	Woodman	2/	—

The remainder of the Works of Mr. James will be published in Monthly Volumes at 2s. each.

Paper Covers.	Limp Cl. Gilt.		Picture Boards.	Hf. Roan.
		HOOTON, Charles—		
—	—	Colin Clink	2/	—
		KINGSLEY, Henry—		
—	—	Stretton	2/	—
		KINGSTON, W. H. G.—		
—	—	Albatross	2'	—
—	—	The Pirate of the Mediterranean...	2'	—
		LANG, John—		
—	—	Ex-Wife	2/	—
—	—	Will He Marry Her?	2/	—
		LEVER, Charles—		
—	—	Arthur O'Leary	2'	2 6
—	—	Con Cregan	2'	2.6
		LE FANU, Sheridan—		
—	—	Torlogh O'Brien	2'	—
		LONG, Lady Catherine—		Cloth.
—	—	First Lieutenant	2/	2 6
—	—	Sir Roland Ashton	2/	2 6
		LOVER, Samuel—		Hf. Roan.
—	—	Handy Andy	2/	2 6
—	—	Rory O'More	2/	2 6
—	—	**LYTTON, Right Hon. Lord—**		Cloth.
—	—	Alice: Sequel to Ernest Maltravers	2/	2,6
—	—	Caxtons	2/	2 6
—	—	Devereux	2/	2 6
—	—	Disowned	2/	2 6
—	—	Ernest Maltravers	2/	2.6
—	—	Eugene Aram	2/	2,6
—	—	Godolphin...	2'	2 6
—	—	Harold	2/	2 6
—	—	The Last of the Barons	2/	2,6
—	—	Leila	2'	2,6
—	—	The Pilgrims of the Rhine		
—	—	Lucretia	2/	2/6
—	—	My Novel, vol. 1...	2/	2/6
—	—	Do. vol. 2...	2/	2/6
—	—	Night and Morning	2/	2/6

Paper Covers.	Limp Cl. Gilt.		Picture Boards.	Cloth Gilt.

LYTTON, LORD—*continued.*

—	—	Paul Clifford	2/	2/6
—	—	Pelham	2/	2/6
—	—	Pompeii, The Last Days of ...	2/	2/6
—	—	Rienzi	2/	2/6
—	—	Strange Story	2/	2/6
—	—	What will He Do with It? vol. 1	2/	2/6
—	—	Do. do. vol. 2	2/	2/6
—	—	Zanoni	2/	2/6

Sets of Lord Lytton's Novels, 22 vols., fcap. 8vo, cloth, £2 15s.; boards, £2 4s. (*See also page* 19.)

MAILLARD, Mrs.—

1/	—	Adrien	—	—
1/	—	Compulsory Marriage	—	—
1/	—	Zingra the Gipsy	—	—

MAXWELL, W. H.—   Hf. Roan.

—	—	The Bivouac	2/	2/6
—	—	Brian O'Linn ; or, Luck... ...	2/	2/6
—	—	Captain Blake	2/	2/6
—	—	Captain O'Sullivan	2/	2/6
—	—	Flood and Field	2/	2/6
—	—	Hector O'Halloran	2/	2/6
—	—	Stories of the Peninsular War ...	2/	2/6
1/	1/6	Stories of Waterloo	2/	2/6
—	—	Wild Sports in the Highlands ...	2/	2/6
—	—	Wild Sports in the West ...	2/	2/6

The Set, in 10 vols., half roan, £1 5s.

MARK TWAIN—

(*See* "AMERICAN LIBRARY," *page* 23).

MARRYAT, Captain—   Cl. Gilt.

The New Edition, with 6 Original Illustrations. (*See page* 19.)

1/	1/6	Dog Fiend	2/	2/6
1/	1/6	Frank Mildmay	2/	2/6
1/	1/6	Jacob Faithful	2/	2/6
1/	1/6	Japhet in Search of a Father ...	2/	2/6
1/	1/6	King's Own	2/	2/6
1/	1/6	Midshipman Easy	2/	2/6
1/	1/6	Monsieur Violet	—	—
1/	1/6	Newton Forster	2/	2/6

Paper Covers.	Limp Cl. Gilt.		Picture Boards.	Cloth Gilt.
		MARRYAT, CAPTAIN—*continued.*		
1/	1/6	Olla Podrida	—	—
1/	1/6	Percival Keene	2/	2 6
1/	1/6	Phantom Ship	2/	2 6
1/	1/6	Poacher	2/	2 6
1/	1/6	Pacha of Many Tales	2/	2 6
1/	1/6	Peter Simple	2/	2 6
1/	1/6	Rattlin the Reefer	2/	2 6
1/	1/6	Valerie	—	—

The Set of Captain Marryat's Novels, 16 vols. bound in 8, cloth, £1 5s.; 16 vols. cloth, £1 4s.; paper, 16s.; 13 vols. (steel plates), cloth, £1 12s. 6d.

				Hf. Roan.
		MARTINEAU, Harriet—		
—	—	The Hour and the Man	2/	2 6
		MAYHEW, Brothers—		
—	—	The Greatest Plague of Life ...	2/	2 6
—	—	Whom to Marry and How to Get Married	2/	2/6

These two Works have Steel Plates by George Cruikshank.

		MILLER, Thomas—		
—	—	Gideon Giles, the Roper... ...	2/	—
		MORIER, Captain—		
—	—	Hajji Baba in Ispahan	2/	—
—	—	Zohrab the Hostage	2/	—
		NEALE, Capt. W. J.—		
—	—	Captain's Wife	2/	—
—	—	Cavendish	2/	—
—	—	Flying Dutchman	2/	—
—	—	Gentleman Jack	2/	—
—	—	The Lost Ship	2/	—
—	—	Port Admiral	2/	—
1/	—	Pride of the Mess	—	—
		NORTON, The Hon. Mrs.—		
—	—	Stuart of Dunleath	2/	—
		OLD SAILOR—		
—	—	Land and Sea Tales	2/	—
—	—	Top-Sail Sheet-Blocks	2/	—
—	—	Tough Yarns	2/	—
—	—	The War-Lock	2/	—

Paper Covers.	Limp Cl. Gilt.		Picture Boards.	Hf. Roan.
		POOLE, John—		
—	—	Phineas Quiddy	2/	—
		PORTER, Jane—		
—	—	The Pastor's Fireside	2/	2/6
—	—	The Scottish Chiefs	2/	2/6
—	—	Thaddeus of Warsaw	2/	2/6
		3 vols., half roan, 7s. 6d.		
•		**RICHARDSON, Samuel—**		Cloth.
—	—	Clarissa Harlowe...	2/6	3/6
—	—	Pamela	2/6	3/6
—	—	Sir Charles Grandison	2/6	3/6
		The Set, 3 vols., 10s. 6d., cloth.		
		ROSS, Charles H.—		
1/	—	A Week with Mossoo	—	—
		SAUNDERS, Captain Patten—		Hf.Roan.
—	—	Black and Gold: A Tale of Circassia	2/	2/6
		SCOTT, Lady—		
—	—	Marriage in High Life	2/	—
1/	1/6	Henpecked Husband	—	—
—	—	The Pride of Life...	2/	—
—	—	Trevelyan	2/	—
		SKETCHLEY, Arthur—		
—	—	Mrs. Brown on the Shah's Visit	1/	—
—	—	Mrs. Brown on the Liquor Law	1/	—
—	—	Mrs. Brown on the Alabama Case	1/	—
—	—	Mrs. Brown on the Tichborne Case	1/	—
—	—	Mrs. Brown on the Tichborne Defence	1/	—
—	—	Mrs. Brown's 'Oliday Houtings...	1/	—
—	—	Mrs. Brown at the Play	1/	—
—	—	Mrs. Brown on the Grand Tour...	1/	—
—	—	Mrs. Brown in the Highlands ...	1/	—
—	—	Mrs. Brown in London	1/	—
—	—	Mrs. Brown in Paris	1/	—
—	—	Mrs. Brown at the Sea-side ...	1/	—
—	—	Mrs. Brown in America	1/	—
—	—	The Brown Papers, 1st Series ...	1/	—
—	—	The Brown Papers, 2nd Series ...	1/	—

Paper Covers.	Limp Cl. Gilt.		Picture Boards.	Cloth.

SKETCHLEY, ARTHUR—*continued*.

—	—	Miss Tompkins' Intended ...	1/	—
—	—	Out for a Holiday	1/	—
—	—	Mrs. Brown on Woman's Rights	1/	—

Mrs. Brown on the Battle of Dorking, paper covers, **6d.**

SMEDLEY, Frank E.—

—	—	The Colville Family ...	2/	3/
—	—	Frank Fairleigh	2 6	3 6
—	—	Harry Coverdale	2 6	3 6
—	—	Lewis Arundel	3	4

The Set, in 4 vols., **14s.**

SMITH, Albert—

Hf. Roan.

—	—	Christopher Tadpole ...	2	2 6
—	—	Marchioness of Brinvilliers ...	2	2 6
—	—	Mr. Ledbury's Adventures ...	2	2 6
—	—	The Pottleton Legacy ...	2	2 6
—	—	The Scattergood Family... ...	2,	2 6

The Set of Albert Smith's Novels, in 5 vols., half roan, 12s. **6d.**; 5 vols., boards, **10s.**

SMOLLETT, Tobias—

—	—	Humphrey Clinker	2/	2 6
—	—	Peregrine Pickle	2/	2 6
—	—	Roderick Random	2,	2 0

The Set of 3 vols., half roan, **7s. 6d.**

STERNE, Laurence—

1/	—	{ Tristram Shandy, and { Sentimental Journey ...	{ —	—

STRETTON, Hesba—

—	—	The Clives of Burcot	2/	2 6

SUE, Eugene—

—	—	The Mysteries of Paris	2/	2 6
—	—	The Wandering Jew	2/	2/6

THOMAS, Annie—

—	—	False Colours	2/	—
—	—	Sir Victor's Choice	2/	—

VIDOCQ—

—	—	The French Police Spy	2/	—

Paper Covers.	Limp Cl. Gilt.		Picture Boards.	Cloth.
		WETHERELL, Elizabeth—		
—	—	Ellen Montgomery's Book Case	2/	2/6
—	—	Melbourne House	2/	2/6
1/	1/6	My Brother's Keeper	—	—
—	—	The Old Helmet	2/	2/6
—	—	Queechy	2/	2/6
—	—	The Two Schoolgirls, and other Tales	2/	2/6
—	—	The Wide, Wide World... ...	2/	2/6

		" Whitefriars," Author of—	Ill. Roan.	
—	—	Cæsar Borgia	2/	2/6
—	—	Gold Worshippers	2/	2/6
—	—	Madeline Graham	2/	2/6
—	—	Maid of Orleans	2/	2/6
—	—	Owen Tudor	2/	2/6
—	—	Westminster Abbey	2/	2/6
—	—	Whitefriars	2/	2/6
—	—	Whitehall	2/	2/6
		The Set of 8 vols., half bound, 20s.		

		TROLLOPE, Mrs.—		
—	—	The Barnabys in America ...	2/	2/6
—	—	One Fault	2/	2/6
—	—	Petticoat Government	2/	2/6
—	—	The Ward...	2/	2/6
—	—	Widow Barnaby	2/	2/6
—	—	The Widow Married	2/	2/6

		YATES, Edmund—		
—	—	Kissing the Rod	2/	2/6
—	—	Running the Gauntlet	2/	2/6

		Anonymous—		
—	—	Bashful Irishman...	2/	—
—	—	Dr. Goethe's Courtship	2/	—
—	—	Guy Livingstone...	2/	—
—	—	Lewell Pastures	2/	—
—	—	Manœu' ing Mother	2/	—
1/	—	The Old Commodore	—	—
—	—	Outward Bound	2/	2/6
1/	—	Violet the Danseuse	—	—
—	—	Who is to Have It ?	2/	—
—	—	The Young Curate	2/	—

www.ingramcontent.com/pod-product-compliance
Lightning Source LLC
Chambersburg PA
CBHW020756020726
47495CB00008B/2452